T0286901

TO THE
KENNELS

ALSO BY HYE-YOUNG PYUN

The Hole
City of Ash and Red
The Law of Lines
The Owl Cries

TO THE KENNELS

AND OTHER STORIES

HYE-YOUNG PYUN

Translated from the Korean by

SORA KIM-RUSSELL AND

HEINZ INSU FENKL

ARCADE PUBLISHING • NEW YORK

First English-language Edition

This is a work of fiction. Names, places, characters, and incidents are either the products of the author's imagination or are used fictitiously.

Originally published in Korean under the title 사육장 쪽으로 (Sayukjang jjogeuro) by Munhak Dongne. The translations in this edition are based on the second edition of the original Korean text.

This book was translated and published with the support of a generous grant from the Daesan Foundation, Seoul.

Arcade Publishing books may be purchased in bulk at special discounts for sales promotion, corporate gifts, fundraising, or educational purposes. Special editions can also be created to specifications. For details, contact the Special Sales Department, Arcade Publishing, 307 West 36th Street, 11th Floor, New York, NY 10018 or arcade@skyhorsepublishing.com.

Arcade Publishing® is a registered trademark of Skyhorse Publishing, Inc.®, a Delaware corporation.

Visit our website at www.arcadepub.com.

10 9 8 7 6 5 4 3 2 1

Library of Congress Cataloging-in-Publication Data

Names: P'yŏn, Hye-yŏng, 1972- author. | Kim-Russell, Sora, translator. | Fenkl, Heinz Insu, 1960- translator.
Title: To the kennels : and other stories / Hye-young Pyun ; translated from the Korean by Sora Kim-Russell, Heinz Insu Fenkl. Other titles: Sayukchang tchok ŭro. English Description: First English-language edition. | New York : Arcade Publishing, 2024. | Summary: "Six elephants bolt from an amusement park and vanish; where they're found brings back memories of a forgotten dictator. A car ride on a foggy highway at night becomes a drive through hell for a young couple getting away for the weekend together. A family lives the dream of moving from the city to a brand-new bedroom town in the country, only to be plagued by debt and fears of eviction, while the sound of incessant barking rings from the kennels nearby. In a city built on the site of ancient tombs, a homeowner's renovation of a broken wall leads to an outcome no one expected. Older workers hired to play characters from a folk tale and wear smiles no one believes. An accountant asked to cook the books for his boss. A would-be writer disapppointed in her students and her choices. These are some of the premises and characters in Hye-young Pyun's To the Kennels, winner of one of Korea's most prestigious literary awards. Infused with psychological acuity, understated suspense, a touch of the uncanny, and her Kafkaesque take on the contemporary world, To the Kennels offers a thrilling, unsettling ride through territory that is both familiar and strange. As Un-su Kim, author of The Plotters has observed, she "reveals to us the cellular division of emotions we've never seen before.""-- Provided by publisher. Identifiers: LCCN 2024019627 (print) | LCCN 2024019628 (ebook) | ISBN 9781956763669 (hardcover) | ISBN 9781648210617 (ebook) Subjects: LCGFT: Short stories. Classification: LCC PL994.67.H94 S2913 2024 (print) | LCC PL994.67.H94 (ebook) | DDC 895.73/5--dc23/eng/20240627 LC record available at https://lccn.loc.gov/2024019627 LC ebook record available at https://lccn.loc.gov/2024019628

Cover design by David Ter-Avanesyan and Erin Seaward-Hiatt
Cover illustration: Getty Images

Printed in the United States of America

CONTENTS

TO THE
KENNELS

THE TRIP

The fog settled even more thickly after they passed the tollgate. Cars were moving slowly as if the road were covered in ice. There had been a fourteen-car pileup on the main Han River bridge not long ago: twelve dead, thirty-nine injured—a major accident. It was because of the fog.

The man slowed gradually and pulled to the side of the road. He wanted to check the map again so they wouldn't get lost. Dense fog wrapped itself around the stopped car.

"This is the road we should take."

With his finger, the man indicated the road. On the surface of the map, it seemed to go on forever. In reality, it would be much more complicated than what was shown there. Maps are always simpler than reality.

The woman felt a twinge of motion sickness just looking at the yellow lines.

The man turned on the radio and tuned in to the traffic station. Between one upbeat song and the following one, an announcer warned of thick fog with visibility of less than fifty yards. The woman leaned close to the windshield and peered at the road they would have to follow.

She didn't know how long it had been since she'd taken a trip like this. Every time they planned one, something would come up for one of them. Last month, it was the man's college reunion. He'd said lots of his senior classmates were coming who had established themselves as soccer coaches. If he played his cards right, he might make a connection that would lead to one of those jobs, and besides, he didn't want to regret not having been there with the other guys. The month before, they hadn't been able to go because of the woman. She'd been so sick she could hardly stand. Full of regret, they'd postponed the trip. It was hard to find a weekend when neither of them was sick or busy. She couldn't just reschedule her classes to take a vacation.

Her students learned a lot more from her than composition, and it wasn't easy to arrange a joint makeup session at a school where kids each had their own schedule. She had no choice but to set aside time for them individually. Since you always come back from a trip at least twice as tired, they'd have to spend at least a week away to make it worthwhile.

"I don't get a sense of how far it is from the map," the woman said, holding her queasy stomach.

"Maps are like that. But isn't it neat? We're smaller than this tiny dot printed here."

What the man pointed to as a dot was actually a symbol representing a school.

The woman gave a faint smile, but she was thinking this was no fun at all. The man used childish old clichés as if he'd come up with them himself. The woman thought it would be an adventure to take a road she hadn't ever been on before using only a map. The road extended in various directions like tiny branches.

Every year, new roads would appear on this route, and they could be wider or narrower. There must have been roads that had disappeared altogether, too. The man's map had been issued six years ago; they'd been using it since he first started driving. There was no way to know how much the roads had changed during all that time.

The woman wedged herself deeper in her seat. It seemed as though the front passenger seat had been pulled forward a little more than it used to be. She had felt a bit cramped when she first got into the car. She used to be able to stretch her legs comfortably, but now she had to bend her knees a little.

"I couldn't possibly have gotten taller," the woman mumbled.

"What?" the man said.

He seemed distracted. It was the man who had picked the date, decided on their destination, and booked the lodgings. He started to hum through his nose.

"What do you think?" he said. "You're finally getting away."

The woman was uncomfortable and didn't say anything in response.

"Huh?"

The man turned to the woman, waiting for an answer.

"Why did it have to be foggy . . . ?"

The woman was blaming the fog for no apparent reason. It was obvious someone else had been sitting in the front seat. The woman squirmed as if she wanted the man to look at her.

"The fog's fine," the man said. "It means tomorrow will be sunny. There won't be a trace of it in the morning."

In W City there was a mountain with organic tea plantations. And at the edge of the city was the ocean, with a meandering coastline and cruise ships that followed it. "It's a spot where you don't have to worry about whether you want to be down at the shore or up in the mountains."

That's what the man had said when he picked the place. He was sitting in the driver's seat, wiping the windshield with a dry rag. But no matter how much he wiped, the pale fog didn't go away.

They'd met in front of the woman's house at ten o'clock that night. It would take around six hours from the tollgate to get to W City. From the woman's house, that would make it almost seven hours. The woman had terrible motion sickness. Ocean, mountain, valley, it made no difference. She just wished where they were going was closer to home.

The very thought of being in a car for seven hours made her terribly dizzy.

"You know, they did a survey of people in Seoul last year," the man said as he eased the car forward. "W City was the number one choice for hidden tourist attractions. I mean, you've got to go to a place like that at least once in your life."

When the man had first asked about going on a trip, the woman too had dreamed of a night far from the city. But by the time they were about to leave, she'd changed her mind and wished she could just eat her fill of jumbo shrimp from the coast nearby. She didn't really have time to take two days off. Besides, she couldn't stand the motion sickness.

"It'll take seven hours," the woman said. "Do we really have to go *there*?"

The man replied as if the answer were perfectly obvious to a man.

"That's what makes it feel like you've been on a trip, right?"

"If I could just have some jumbo shrimp," the woman mumbled.

"You can have jumbo shrimp there!" the man shouted. He was quick-tempered, and his tone was harsh. He was easy to anger but also quick to let go.

"You know I get carsick easily," the woman said defensively.

The man's reply was curt: "Take your medication."

The woman shut her mouth.

They had stopped by a supermarket before leaving Seoul. The place had been packed with people enjoying their night shopping. The woman put bottled water and two net bags of tangerines in her cart. She also picked up some Fuji apples that were nicely uniform in color. At the food counter, she bought several uncut sushi rolls that cost two thousand won apiece.

"If we'd known, we could have made sushi," the man said, giving the woman a look.

She pretended not to hear and picked out some snacks. Cookies and candy. She selected three six-packs of canned beer, all different brands, a package of fries, and day-old bread that was on sale. She also bought travel tissues and two pairs of socks she'd forgotten to bring. And she didn't omit dried squid and peanuts to munch on. The man bought two and a half pounds of pork belly at the meat department.

"They'll have it there," the woman said.

Her criticism was lost in the sound of the man's footsteps as he headed to the produce section. He filled plastic bags with lettuce and chicory.

"Buying some meat makes it feel like a picnic, doesn't it?" the man said.

5

Instead of answering, the woman massaged the bag of pork belly. It felt cold and squishy.

On the way to check out, the woman regarded herself in a mirror. She knew it would be cold early in the morning and she had worn a down jacket, but now she saw it made her body look thick. She was unhappy with the weather these days, which was unseasonably warm for early winter. She wanted to go home and change into lighter clothing, but then she didn't know if the man would want to forget about the trip and suggest they just check into a motel. The woman hurried over to the clothing department.

The man stood with his arms crossed and a disapproving expression.

"At this rate, we'll be late," he said.

The woman knew he wasn't very patient. Quickly scanning between the hangers, she didn't see anything she liked. She wouldn't have been able to buy anything, even if she did like it. The man's expression had hardened.

As they passed the tollgate, the woman exclaimed suddenly, "Oh, my motion sickness medicine!"

Rushing to finish her class so they could leave, she'd been distracted and hadn't packed her medication. At the supermarket, she'd been preoccupied with the clothes and had forgotten to buy some. The man just turned, gave the woman a glance, and said nothing. It wasn't clear whether he was upset with her. As soon as she realized she didn't have her medication, the inside of the car became unbearably stuffy. She started to sweat under her turtleneck. The cheap angora made her body itch, and she scratched herself here and there underneath where her hands could reach.

"Why don't you just take the sweater off?" the man said.

"Here?"

Even as she asked, she thought, If not here, then where else would she take it off? The fog would hide everything.

In fog like this, no one would notice even if she were naked.

The car moved slowly forward, dispersing the fog. The taillights of the car ahead of them were like a security beacon illuminating the road. The woman pressed her body deep into her seat. Wearing only a camisole on top, she covered herself using the goose down jacket like a blanket and silently watched the fog roll back in.

The woman taught composition to more than twenty children. She didn't get off work until after nine at night and even later on days when she had meetings with parents. During her school years, when she was younger, there had been several occasions when she'd won awards for her writing. She'd once won first prize in the prose writing division.

She received the award directly from the mayor, who reached out to shake hands, her palms damp with sweat. When the woman was in college, the mayor ran for a seat in the National Assembly. She voted for that candidate without a second thought. The mayor had beaten the opposition candidate by a narrow margin and become a member of the assembly, but after her term ended, she wasn't reelected because she'd been involved in several scandals during her tenure. She would have retired from politics by now. Some of the woman's awards were still at her parents' house. The one she'd received from the mayor had created an opportunity, and she'd been able to enroll in the creative arts department at a university in the city.

No matter how much she taught them, the children never

developed a feel for writing. Every sentence they wrote was the same, and when she asked them to write a sentence with only a subject and an object, they asked her what a subject was, and that depressed her.

The woman spent much of her time writing essays and other pieces for students to submit to writing contests. It was hard for her if at least one of them wasn't a winner. The more winners the better. At the school, it was also usually the woman's job to assign book reports as homework and provide topics for writing exercises related to basic life skills. She was generally fond of the children but not the ones who didn't know something as simple as the difference between a subject and an object. And when June came around, she didn't care for the ones who composed anticommunist posts declaring how much they hated communism—or who wrote that they wanted their hearts to be as pure as the clear blue sky. She didn't like the ones who wrote that they would become future celebrities, and she didn't like the ones who begged her to let them write *anything at all* because the future had no hope for them. All those students of hers.

The man yawned as if he were sleepy. For the last month, he'd been working at an apartment construction job by the river without a single day off. For a while before that, he'd been unemployed. The man had been on the soccer team at the woman's college. He was a striker, but he hadn't actually gotten to play in many games. By graduation, he hadn't been signed by anyone, and he decided belatedly he was more suited for defense. Instead of bemoaning the time he'd wasted on his athletic talent, he jumped at the chance to work at apartment construction jobs and, fortunately, he liked the work. The woman felt it a pity the man went into manual labor without even trying anything else. On the other hand, she thought he possessed a certain dignity for not declining such work.

When his supervisor wasn't looking, the man would take the opportunity to sneak a long piss into the cement poured by the mixer truck. It wasn't exactly malicious.

The higher the floor, the harder it was to go down and then back up again and again to go to the bathroom, so the supports and the walls of bedrooms and living rooms in the apartments were constructed with urine-saturated concrete. The residents would sleep with their beds against piss-soaked walls. Entire families would gather to watch dramas on the wall-mounted TVs. The higher the floor, the greater the quantity of urine mixed in with the concrete. A few of the other workers had started secretly pissing together too. They would laugh and piss into the wet concrete unseen by the foreman.

As the car slowed, the woman's stomach churned. She took a tangerine from one of the shopping bags she'd placed on the back seat. The tangerine had already lost its freshness, but the woman put a lukewarm piece in her mouth anyway. They had longed for the sort of life that would allow them to drive out of the city on weekends. So this trip wasn't so much a sudden thing as their long-cherished wish finally come to fruition. The woman hadn't even gone backpacking—which was a common thing when they were in college—because she'd had to work part-time all the way through school. It was the same for the man. He had never been on a trip except to the soccer team's training camp in a southern province. The woman wanted to call her friends and brag about going to W City even though she found the trip an annoyance.

None of her friends had been there yet. She began to feel sorry about having suddenly insisted on eating jumbo shrimp locally.

Somehow, it was already past midnight. Fog still obscured the road, and if not for the taillights of the car ahead, she would have believed they were driving through hell and not on the highway.

Occasionally, there were large vehicles—trucks and tractor trailers—going fast, cutting through the thick fog. They drove without slowing down, regardless of the fog. The woman opened the window a crack to soothe her stomach, and the fog seeped in with the cold wind. The fog itself was warm, and yet she got goose bumps under the jacket. The man said something, but the wind was so loud she couldn't hear him properly. To avoid motion sickness, it helps to keep one's eyes focused at a distance, but in the darkness the only things visible were the faint outlines of mountains and factory buildings.

"Close the window. I can't stand the noise," the man said.

The woman dry heaved, as if to say, *Look at me*. The man just nagged her to drink some water. His upbeat mood seemed to have come down quite a lot from the fog. Because of her motion sickness, the woman decided to take a nap, but sleep wouldn't come. She usually went to bed in the morning and woke after noon since her work didn't start till 4:00 p.m. Her heart was pounding now, perhaps because of the strong coffee she'd been drinking while teaching her class that day. The man, on the other hand, couldn't fight off his drowsiness. He nodded off and then, startled, opened his eyes wide. He'd swung by to pick the woman up as soon as he got off work. It was a twenty-eight-floor apartment building, and he'd been working on the eighth floor that day. The woman felt some sympathy for the man. She peeled a tangerine and put it in his mouth. He munched on it, leaking some of the juice.

The lights of the rest area were a pale glow in the fog. The man reclined his seat, thinking he would close his eyes for a moment. The woman pulled the zipper up to tidy the front of the goose down jacket she wore over her camisole. In the middle of the night, the rest area wasn't as quiet as one would have expected. The woman bought a flesh-colored motion sickness patch about the size of a fingernail and stuck it behind her ear. There wasn't much use applying it now. A patch-type medication had to be applied at least four hours ahead to be effective. When she put on the patch, she heard a high-pitched humming sound like an insect vibrating its wings in her narrow ear canal. She covered her ears with her hands, but the sound didn't stop.

The woman bought some ice cream to soothe her stomach and sat at a table by herself. A man carrying a tray of food casually walked over and sat next to her. He reeked of diesel fuel.

"Hey, big sis, where you goin'?" he asked.

He smiled at her. She looked at him, thinking he might be someone she knew, but he was a stranger. She regarded him carefully and noticed he was cute. Handsome face. The woman put ice cream in her mouth.

"What makes you say I'm your big sister?" she said. "So where are *you* going, little brother?"

He said he was driving a twenty-five-ton tanker to T City, where there was a port.

"How does it feel driving a truck like that?"

"There's only two things you gotta watch out for speeding

down the highway at night—tanker trucks and women," the man answered, pointing at her.

The woman gave an amused laugh. She didn't know what was so funny, but she kept laughing.

"You want a ride? You can go down to T City with me," the man replied with a smile when the woman said she'd never been in a big rig. She scooped up her leftover ice cream and ate it all at once, with a wide grin.

"Do you get carsick in a truck like that?" she said.

"It's worse. The whole world spins around."

The woman burst out laughing again, revealing all the melted ice cream inside her mouth. The man dipped rice in his beef bone soup and ate a spoonful.

"Where are you goin', big sis?"

"W City."

"What for?"

"What for? Taking a trip, of course."

"You must be makin' a good living, takin' a trip and all."

The woman wanted to show off a bit.

"That's not why," she said. "I mean, who doesn't go on trips these days?"

The man just grunted but didn't say much else.

Watching the man put another spoonful of rice in his mouth, the woman felt famished. She crumpled her empty ice cream container and stood.

"See you at the next rest stop," the man said, spooning hot soup into his mouth this time. "I'll be waiting for you."

He waved, still holding the rice-specked spoon in his hand. The woman thought he was uncouth, but she waved back.

She left the customer service area. She had forgotten where the car was parked—it was frustrating. All the cars were hard to make out in the fog. After wandering around looking for a long time, she finally found the man's. He was asleep, snoring lightly. The woman got in next to him and ate the cold sushi. As she chewed, she thought she should have asked the young truck driver how far it was to the next rest stop. Would he really be waiting for her there? The woman smiled at the uncertainty and the anticipation of it, then shook the man to wake him.

"At this rate, are you planning to get there in the middle of the afternoon?" she said.

As soon as he opened his eyes, the man took the sushi from the woman's hand and put it in his mouth. He went to the bathroom, and the woman randomly ate the snacks and cookies she'd bought at the supermarket until he returned. She even ate all the fries, which had gone cold and limp, but that didn't satisfy her hunger. She watched the faint lights of the cars on the highway, regretting that the young man's tanker truck was hidden in the fog,

"How far is it to the next rest stop?" she asked.

"You should have gone to the bathroom," the man snapped at her.

She wanted to fire back at him that if he kept treating her this way he wouldn't see her again after the next rest stop. But she restrained herself. She knew she couldn't stay angry like this forever. She didn't want it to be that way again. The fog descended, as firmly as the woman's closed mouth.

There was nothing to do but slowly follow the car in front, as if the road would go on forever. Road signs weren't visible because they were obscured by the fog. The woman unfolded the map.

"Where the hell are we?"

The man pointed to part of the map with his finger.

"Around here."

"So where is *here*?" the woman asked.

As if annoyed, the man read out loud the place name indicated by his finger. It didn't sound familiar, but it wasn't far from the city they'd started out from.

"Look, don't those lights look just like moonlight?" the man asked.

The woman was lost in her thoughts. She wanted to correct what the man had said with a red pen. She wanted to tell him not to use a simile unless he was writing a novel. All the similes in the world were generally clichés already, so unless you were writing for humor, it was better not to make careless analogies. But instead of saying any of this, the woman nodded at the man. There was no way he was going to fix the way he spoke overnight.

Tomorrow, some of the woman's students would be participating in a writing contest. One of them had to win to keep enrollments from declining. The woman had made up her mind to ask for an increase in her students' fees starting next month, but it concerned her when she remembered how they filled everything they wrote with clichés no matter how much she taught them. Their starting every sentence with a first-person subject worried her. Her indifference when she saw them misbehaving worried her. And it worried her that—even while claiming she would highlight their strong points—she praised bad writing and expressions not entirely appropriate coming from a child.

A long, snakelike tractor trailer rattled past the car.

"How long to the rest stop?" the woman asked again.

"Around thirty minutes? It seems urgent."

After looking her over from top to bottom, his eyes fixated on her ear. Suddenly, he burst out laughing.

"You put on a motion sickness patch," he said. "When I see someone with one of those, they look like a kid in elementary school. It makes me laugh."

The woman flipped her hair from behind her ear over to the front. Her headache made her head feel leaden. To settle her stomach, she closed her eyes and lay back in her seat.

The man slowed and pulled onto the shoulder.

"Get out and pee," he said.

The woman hesitated. No matter how urgent it was, she had no intention of hiding in the fog to piss.

"Be quick about it," the man urged her.

Reluctantly, she got out of the car and lowered her pants toward the guard rail. The fog was unexpectedly warm on her bare bottom, and though she didn't actually need to, she peed for a long time, the fog melting away as she relieved herself.

She found herself thinking that if lots of people got together to pee like this, they could dissolve all the fog. It was a funny thought, and that made her embarrassment subside a little. The woman pulled up her pants and then, as she was getting back into the car, stopped, startled.

The man had been standing by the headlights the whole time, smoking and watching her pee. The cigarette smoke was masked by fog. Maybe it was the headlights illuminating him while the thick fog hid his legs, but he looked like a dead man floating up to heaven.

*

While the woman had her eyes closed, the man passed the rest area. She wasn't sleeping—she'd only closed her eyes.

"I told you to stop," she said.

The sign for the rest area receded behind them.

"You have to go again?" the man said.

The woman was furious at the man for criticizing her need to use the bathroom. The idea that he wasn't respecting what she said began to drive her crazy. She felt an overwhelming anger inside her.

She wanted to rain curses on him, but what actually came out was vomit. The man fumbled about, then held out a bag from the supermarket. The woman couldn't hold it in, throwing up everything inside, and opened her window to get rid of the smell. The thick fog outside seeped into the car, and the man coughed from the cold air. The woman's stomach seemed to have settled a bit. She thrust her face out the window to catch the cold wind to her heart's content. The man yelled at her to throw the bag out.

"It's just fog anyway," he said. "No one's going to see."

The woman pretended not to hear. Getting rid of the smell wasn't going to be easy. Even so, she didn't want to just mindlessly toss the bag out the window. She tied the end tight and set the bag down carefully on the back seat. The man couldn't tolerate the cold wind and closed his window.

"Damn it!" he exclaimed, suddenly slamming on the brakes.

The taillights of a huge vehicle were flashing directly in front of them. The woman almost banged her head, but luckily her goose down jacket provided a cushion. The man began to swear and pulled onto the shoulder. Staying on the roadway could lead to a whole chain of collisions. The man motioned the driver of the vehicle in front to pull over, but it just sped off. Its license plate was hard to make out in the fog. It was clearly a large vehicle, though exactly how large wasn't obvious. The woman pressed her face close to the windshield and saw it was a tanker truck with an oval-shaped tank.

Maybe it's the truck the young man I met at the rest stop is driving, she thought. It couldn't possibly be, but then maybe it could be—she was ambivalent.

"It's easy to drive a truck because other drivers don't bother you. They know they're gonna die if they bump into me. Doesn't matter what's inside," the young man said with a grin.

"What's inside?"

"Gas. Very toxic," he said, snickering.

The tanker truck could have been labeled with a hazardous chemicals warning symbol. The woman felt a sudden chill and gathered her jacket to her. The man spewed curses at the truck as it disappeared into the fog.

They hadn't gone very far before the tanker truck reappeared, this time speeding directly alongside them. Every time the man tried to change lanes, it edged closer. When he did manage just barely to change lanes, the truck followed them and changed lanes too. The more erratic the car's movements, the worse the woman's motion sickness became. It seemed as if they and the truck were the only vehicles on the road. The fog didn't show the least sign of clearing as it pressed its weight down on their speeding forms.

After jockeying with the truck for some time, the man exited the main highway onto a national byway. The truck continued to speed down the highway, unable to follow.

"Won't it take longer if we go this way?" the woman managed to ask, her mind a blur from motion sickness.

"We can get off and then get back on the highway in a little while," the man replied. "I didn't want to get into a stupid accident fighting with a truck like that."

He seemed relieved as he pulled onto the dark road. The darkness even seemed to dissipate the fog a bit, but they might have been better off staying in it—the national road was surrounded by black mountains without a single light. It was so dark and silent the silence became frightening. They were driving solely by the light of their headlights. There was no sound except the faint rumbling of their own tires, and no cars behind them, and yet the man continued to glance at the side mirror. The woman took out a beer and drank it to settle her queasy stomach. But no matter how much she drank, she was still thirsty. She took the pork belly from the black shopping bag and held it to her chest. The cold raw meat squished against her each time she turned her head to look behind them. The pitch-black darkness seemed to crouch there, watching them.

*

The man drove silently, cutting forward through the darkness, and when he was sure no one was following, he stopped looking behind them. The woman's stomach settled a little. The beer made her have to pee again, but she was determined to hold it until she got to their lodgings. To her relief, signs for W City began to appear.

They had been looking forward to an early morning hike, but now she wanted a nap first. The man did, too, and they readily agreed to go see the ocean when they got up.

They were about to make a left turn where the road split for W City and T City, when a shape suddenly appeared in front of them. The man slammed on the brakes but couldn't stop—the distance was too short—and there was a dull thump as the car struck something. The woman, startled, squeezed her eyes shut. The man froze with his hands clutching the steering wheel. It was so dark outside he couldn't tell what he'd hit. Slowly, he got out of the car. The woman thought they'd hit a person, but maybe not. There was no way anyone would be walking along the road in the dark at that hour. It must have been a stray dog or a wild animal, maybe even a deer—they were known to appear at the roadside. There was even a case when a log had fallen from a truck and slid down a hillside onto a national road.

"It's all right," the woman whispered as if consoling herself. The man was bent over at the waist, dragging whatever he had hit to the side of the road. The woman squeezed her eyes shut again. She didn't want to be implicated in what the man was doing by being a witness to it.

After a while, the man got back into the car. For the woman, the time felt really long, as if he'd been to purgatory and back. She didn't ask what he had just gotten rid of. Whatever he said, she wouldn't have been able to believe him.

Even so, she was waiting for the man to say something—anything. He pulled out a wet wipe, slowly cleaned between his fingers, then turned to the backseat and grabbed the bag full of the woman's vomit. It was tied tight, but the smell still leaked out.

The man stuck the used wipe in the bag. He didn't tell the woman again to toss the bag of vomit out onto the roadside. He didn't even wrinkle his nose at the smell. The woman looked at the man's hand clutching the steering wheel. She didn't want to hold that hand ever again.

They drove in silence down the dark road. Occasionally, lights flashed by. It was that time, very early in the morning, when sleepless old people wake up. The man was glancing at the side mirror again. Perhaps he was checking if any cars were following them, or maybe he was trying to make out what it was he'd disposed of on the roadside.

Taking the highway again, they sped along and turned off onto one of the tiny branch roads, where there was a tollgate. The morning light spread little by little over the patches where the fog had cleared. Now it was time to make the final charge to W City. The man drove at the maximum speed. If he'd been driving that fast all night, they might already have unpacked their luggage at their lodgings on the outskirts of the city. They might have hiked up the mountain shrouded in morning mist. It was all because of the fog. W City would be such a great place that simply being there would instantly wash away the fatigue of driving through the night. The woman would like it so much she might even declare she wanted to go live there when she got old. The man wanted to tell her they should get a house together in a village overlooking the sea.

As they sped along, relieved, a huge tanker truck blocked them. The man had no idea where it had come from. Had it been secretly chasing after them? Could it have been lurking on the side of the road, waiting?

"Damn it!"

The man cursed the truck again. The cab sat so high the driver's face wasn't visible. The man weaved back and forth between lanes to avoid the tanker truck, and each time, the huge mass blocked the man's car. The man thought he had started something terrible and pointless.

"Not one guy who drives a tanker is normal," the man declared, as if to comfort himself. "How could they be when they're driving around in a potential fireball?"

Now they couldn't even escape back onto the side road. If they wanted to get to W City, there was no choice but to keep speeding onward as they were. Helpless, the man tried pulling onto the shoulder, but the tanker followed even there. The woman remembered that the man she'd met at the rest stop had said he was going to T City. If that was the case, then he would have taken another route already. But that was beside the point. The driver blocking them couldn't be the one going to T City. Because the man couldn't make out the license plate in the fog, he couldn't even confirm if the vehicle blocking them was the same. In fact, it might not have been intentionally blocking his car at all. Recklessly crossing lanes and obstructing the cars behind them—that might just be standard practice for the men driving large trucks at night.

Could the tanker driver have been watching from the darkness as he'd dragged the thing he hit off to the side of the road?

The tanker was clinging to them so ferociously there was no mistaking its intention now. The man looked like he might burst into tears at any moment.

"That's why he's following me like this," he said, his lips quivering with anxiety.

The woman didn't want to say anything to comfort the man, so she kept her mouth shut. She didn't know what might come out if she spoke.

Ahead of them was a tollgate for W City. Everything would be fine if they could just get through it. Once they left the highway and entered the city, at least there wouldn't be anyone crossing lanes and interfering with their driving. They wouldn't have to clean up the carcass of some animal that came out of the night and suffered an accident, and they wouldn't have to look behind them in the dark over and over. The man sped up one last time to avoid the tanker truck. But then he was on a curve and it was too late to slow down. The car hit the guardrail.

*

The woman was the first to regain consciousness. The man was leaning back against his headrest as if he were sleeping. Neither of them was bleeding. Raw meat was plastered here and there all over the inside of the car—in the impact, it had flown out of the bag the woman had been holding to her chest. The woman peeled the meat, which had lost its fresh color, from her body. She didn't seem to have any external wounds. Still, from the heavy feeling in her body, she was sure that something must be broken somewhere. But she had no trouble moving.

The car's bumper was badly dented where it hit the guardrail.

The fog had cleared completely, and the sun had come up while they were unconscious. The woman stretched now, after hours of having to resist the urge. Her shoulder was stiff, probably from the impact. Less than a hundred yards away was a tollgate, its lights blinking, and quite a few cars were passing through, though it was early in the morning. But the tanker truck was nowhere in sight.

It might have been waiting for them somewhere, or it might have gone on to T City and the port.

The man woke a short time later. Afraid he might have broken bones, he moved his legs cautiously as he got out of the car. As soon as he'd checked the bumper, he cursed the faceless truck driver. He boasted that he'd memorized the license plate number, but even so, he knew there wasn't much that could be done. He looked hopelessly at the crushed bumper and then called a tow truck.

The woman didn't want to go back to the city in the tow truck with the man, and on impulse she climbed over the guardrail.

There was no way of knowing where she was. She could see the tollgate, but she couldn't tell whether or not it was for W City. A flat area stretched out to the side of the guardrail. It was past harvest time, and the paddy fields were covered in a blanket of straw. She heard the man's annoying voice asking where she was going. She started to say something but instead clamped her mouth shut and went down into the rice paddy. It was an early winter morning, and the earth was hard. The woman looked back occasionally as she walked.

What had he been hiding in the darkness on the roadside in the early morning fog? She called out to the man in a loud voice, but the man didn't look at her. Perhaps he didn't hear.

The woman stood there and waved her hand. It took a long time for the man to see her.

"What was it you killed earlier?"

The man cupped a hand over his ear as if he couldn't hear. A dog barked somewhere. There must have been a village nearby. The woman continued walking toward that invisible village. The road was hard, and the breeze was subtle but cold.

After walking for about an hour, she turned around to look. There was no sign of the man's car.

It appeared he had already left in the tow truck. Not until she saw the car was gone did the woman realize her sweater and bag were in it.

Dangling beside the guardrail the man had crashed into was a plastic bag with the name of a supermarket on it. It was the bag full of her vomit. The woman took it in her hand. She stabbed her other hand into her jacket pocket.

The woman stood still and read the road signs hanging in the air, all for places she was seeing for the first time. The sign gave the name of the city where she would arrive at some time in the future but was mute about where she was at the moment. The woman walked slowly along the shoulder. She saw the tollgate not far ahead.

—Translated by Heinz Insu Fenkl

TO THE KENNELS

When he opened the front door—he was leaving on his way to work in the city—a letter fluttered to the ground. The envelope had been stuck in the doorjamb, and it was crumpled as if someone had tried to force it in. There was a white birdhouse mailbox in front of the house, but the envelope had been stuck in the door as if to draw attention. It was nothing remarkable. What caught his eye was the red print on the envelope. Any other time he would have dismissed it as a flyer from the local pizzeria or a mailer from a new herbologist, but as soon as he saw the red text he knew this was a special kind of letter: an eviction notice.

He slowly picked up the crumpled envelope. The notice meant they could barge into his house any time they wanted. His wife, who had come out to see him off, glanced at the envelope in his hand and immediately gasped. She also knew it was from them. Her face went white. She screamed, *"Aaah!* What do we do now?" Her voice was full of fear, as if she thought they might come charging in right then. Now his mother screamed from her room, not even knowing why his wife had screamed, and his wife grew even more frightened because of the noise. His mother suffered from dementia. She wouldn't stop screaming. He frowned slightly in annoyance.

They had climbed over the fence at night like thieves to stick the notice in the door. They could have been hiding by the newly paved road—the night so dark you could barely see your toes—watching for him to return from work. He looked out at the stretch of new pavement that led to the village entrance as if to stare them down. He couldn't be sure they weren't still there, spying on his family and the anxiety they had caused.

That morning in the village was no different from any other. The heads of the single-story houses got into their cars in unison for the commute to the city. Every day, they got into their cars at approximately the same time and squeezed out of the village. Those who didn't leave then usually couldn't get to work by starting time at 9:00 a.m. The cars carrying the breadwinners disappeared in an orderly line over the new road, and mixed in among them were three or four of the same make, model, and even color as his own. Typically, he would have been among the parade to the freeway. To leave the house at the same time every day, he got up at the same time, and to do that he went to bed every night at around the same time. For him, sleeping, eating, and even sex followed a schedule.

The wives leaned against their fences and waved to their husbands leaving for work, then exchanged greetings with their eyes as they headed inside. After the wives were back in their houses, he continued to glare toward the new road until all the cars were gone. Only a thin, early morning fog from the hills lingered on the new road; there was no sign that the men who had stuck the notice in the door were hiding anywhere. He could see the sound wall of the highway beyond the fog, but the rumbling noise of a vehicle was still clearly audible through it. It was probably an overloaded freight truck or a semi. The new road trembled slightly, as if startled by the noise.

The envelope was thin, like it was empty. He was upset that his daily routine had been ruined by this flimsy envelope. Normally, he would have left the new road and been on the highway by now. He stared at his and his wife's names for a long time—in stiff, bold print—at the bottom of the envelope. The longer he did this, the more unfamiliar the names became, and that made him nervous. The bankruptcy was entirely his fault. He had known a letter notifying them of the eviction would come eventually. Still, now that he had actually received the notice, anger rose within him uncontrollably. Exactly what had he done wrong?

He gripped the envelope and tore it up without checking its contents. His name and address, the red letters of the notice and eviction date, the name of the marshal—all torn to tiny pieces. His startled wife stared at him. His screaming old mother stared at him. His son, clutching his wife's skirt, stared at him. Then, sensing the gravity of the mood, the boy burst into tears without knowing why. His wife patted the boy's back, seeming dumbstruck. No one stopped him. His face must have looked fierce and unapproachable as he'd ripped up the envelope. He must have looked angry, too, and that attitude strangely put his wife at ease. She hadn't noticed his hands shaking as he tore the envelope— she took it to be a sign of his resolve to protect the family. He regretted it immediately, because now there was no way of knowing when the marshals would come barging in. Should he have gone to them and pleaded for the eviction date to be pushed back?

Before he could change his mind, he tossed the fragments into the toilet and flushed. The shreds of the notice were sucked down into the whirlpool with a gulp, and the water cleared once again. He hid his still-trembling hands by shoving them into his pants pockets.

"When are they coming?" his wife asked in a slightly lowered voice. Instead of answering, he opened the living room curtains, revealing the smokestacks that hadn't yet been torn down. The village was built on the site of an abandoned industrial chemicals factory, which had been dismantled to convert the lot to residences, but here and there parts of buildings and smokestacks were still standing. White smoke seemed to rise from one of them. It must have been fog rolling down from the hills or scattered clouds—smoke couldn't be coming from the chimney of an abandoned factory. When the fog lifted, the new road was empty, and in the morning sun he could see the dust floating inside the house. His wife frowned. He was confused—was it because of the sunlight, because he didn't answer, or because of the eviction notice? He shook his head at her, not knowing. She went into the bedroom with a gloomy look on her face. "What's certain," he mumbled—looking at the back of her head, white from the sunlight—"is that we're going to be kicked out of this house very soon."

He had no choice but to accept the fact that he was bankrupt, and—needless to say—flat broke. He also had debts he could never repay in a million years. He could no longer borrow money from his friends, let alone from a bank. And he had no family or relatives he could ask, either. Even if there had been someone, it would have been a nuisance to go into a long-winded explanation of his bankruptcy and then listen to their lectures in order to borrow the money. But even if he could have endured a lecture, he wouldn't be able to borrow any money because . . . Thoughts arose in a jumble; he wanted to prioritize things. "The first thing . . ." he muttered, and realized he hadn't left for work yet. He had to go to work, just like any other day. Self-pitying thoughts like *Do I have to go in on time even on the day I got my eviction notice?* didn't occur to him. The money he earned would all be taken by them, but it was important to stick to routine. He glanced at the clock on the wall. He should be approaching the tollgate by now. It was all because of the notice that he was this late.

"There's probably a little time left before the eviction. I just have to find another house to live in by then," he said as he stuffed his feet into his creased black shoes. The heels were worn out on the inside and made his back hurt after just a few steps. His wife looked at him without a word. He gave her a broad smile. "The process begins with the delivery of the eviction notice, but they have to go through more legal steps to confiscate the assets of the bankruptcy filer," he said. He had no way of knowing when the marshals would appear. But the moment he said this, he was sure the eviction would be delayed and they would find a new place to live in the meantime. It was a ridiculously optimistic thought.

*

He passed by fourteen houses to get to the village entrance. There were a total of twenty-two houses in the village standing along the new road in a gentle curve—so as not to block the light—toward the hills. House #1 was at the entrance, and the numbers got higher as you approached the hills. Mr. Y, the broker who gave tours of the development, said that buyers were flocking in for the beautiful scenery, thanks to those hills behind the village. They weren't very high, but they were enough to attract people from the nearby city to come and forage for hazelnuts and chestnuts. It was nothing but some low hills, though, as far as he was concerned. From the new road, you could see patchy pine groves and bald spots here and there, where small grave mounds stood out like scars. There were probably more graves hidden up there. He didn't much care for those hills. Forests with no distinct paths and with unexpected, hidden graves. Forget about hiking. He was the sort that thought, *What's the point of struggling to get to the top if you're only going to come back down?* He knew this sort of sentiment would make him seem stubborn and simpleminded, so he didn't share it with anyone.

The houses appeared to be made of wood at first glance, but they were actually steel-framed. The cost of steel was much less per square foot than wood, and once a site was selected, it took barely ten days to build the house. With modular materials, construction was just lining up corners and tightening them with screws, fitting the houses together like gigantic Lego blocks. Maybe that was why they all looked the same, like they were mass-produced. Little things, like the placement of windows or the exterior walls, were slightly different if you looked closely, but from a distance they all looked identical: a parasol in a white pebble yard, a low-rising flower bed encircled by a latticed fence, identically sized birdhouse mailboxes standing by a swinging gate. On weekend evenings when the weather was nice, the neighbors would grill the same cuts of meat under their parasols. As they put their lettuce wraps into their mouths, one family would catch the eye of another and give a wave, and only after waving back from under their own parasol—at the same angle and the same number of times—would the neighbors also eat their own.

He had decided to move there because he really wanted a single-family home. Their three-story row house in the city was so crowded it was always bustling with activity. Though he didn't much care for them, he felt special for having hills behind the house. It meant he was actually living in the country, and that they had escaped the city. He knew how hard it was to leave the city. Before moving, he had never lived outside the city, but he had never actually lived downtown, either. Where he was born, where he grew up, where he had started a family—it was all in the suburbs on the outskirts. Never living downtown but never venturing outside the city—that was a typical city person.

Once he left the new road, the sound of dogs barking was especially loud. There were kennels where they bred dogs near the village. Mr. Y had said that since the breeder was unlicensed, the kennels would be shut down by the local authorities and would be gone soon. They had tried to force the kennels to relocate but so far had succeeded only in slowing their growth. His wife was hesitant about the move when she heard, but it didn't concern him. Even if the breeder's dogs were ferocious enough to maul each other to death, they would be no problem unless they were somehow to attack a family. In their cramped cages, the dogs would consume the same feed, sleep and wake at around the same time, be sold off to this place or that at random, and in the end be gruesomely roasted to death. No matter how ferocious, they would never leave the kennels unless they were sold off to be killed or died in their cages. The loud barking might be a problem, but he thought he could endure it. In the city where he had lived all his life, noise—and not quiet—was the norm.

But the dogs' barking was hard to bear. It sounded like every dog at the kennels was barking at once. When one started, it was like hundreds of dogs barking at the same time. The noise never stopped all day. A rumor began to circulate among the residents that they were breeding fighting dogs at the kennels. There were lots of other rumors about the kennels: dogs being starved to make them more vicious, dogs pitted against boars in the same cage. There was a story that the kennels were also a slaughter-house. The dirt there was suspiciously red, and there was a strong smell of blood—proof of the butchering. There was even talk of the kennels' owner living in the village. Maybe that was why wives sometimes asked the women next door what their husbands did for a living. Rumors ran thick, but not one person could say they had been to the kennels. He often turned his head toward the noise. The barking seemed muffled as though the kennels were far away, but it also sounded close, as if they were right next door. But with the noise from passing trucks on the highway and the mechanical sounds from under the floor mingled in, it was hard to guess the precise direction.

It was already past his commute time. Normally, he should have been in his office reading the paper and sipping coffee by now. No coworkers concerned about his lateness called. They probably wouldn't have noticed his empty cubicle because of the high partitions. There was an important meeting scheduled for that morning. He tried to remember what the topic was but couldn't. It was probably written on a Post-it stuck to a corner of his monitor. He realized he was entirely unprepared for the meeting if he couldn't even remember the topic. If he did somehow get to the office in time for the meeting, he wouldn't be able to make any useful suggestions. The department head would probably scold him, asking sarcastically if he wore his head just for show.

The moment he had that thought he became more anxious. He turned the steering wheel, thinking he might change lanes and speed up. Suddenly, he heard loud honking. He quickly returned to his lane. He was one of those cautious drivers who obey the speed limit on the highway. He was afraid of the highway. For some reason, semis and mammoth freight trucks—whose tonnage was anyone's guess—were on the road around the time of his commute. They made a deafening noise. If a truck carrying industrial chemicals or machinery was behind him, he felt a crushing pressure in his chest. He slowed down to the speed limit and someone honked from behind again.

Only after he glanced in his side mirror did he realize that a truck the size of a cruise ship was tailgating him. It soon changed lanes and passed. Watching the rear end of the truck, he let out a sigh of relief; soon after, a semi was following him. He pulled completely off to the side of the road and waited until he could no longer see it. He resumed driving, but a moment later, another truck approached. He had to pull over again. Only after going on and off the shoulder like this several times did he arrive at the tollgates to enter the city.

As he rolled down his window to pay the female attendant, he breathed in the friendly and familiar city air, welcoming it into his lungs. The house he owned in the city was at the north end of the river. Despite problems with microdust, noise pollution, and overcrowding, it was still prime real estate as an investment. In other words, he had once lived in a true city, with blowing dust, unending noise, and jostling crowds. His place was in a residential neighborhood packed with row houses. He had taken out a mortgage to buy a three-story row house. Now he rented to several families—even the basement—but his mortgage payment was still so large he could have covered the floor in 10,000-won bills. He wasn't sure he'd be able to pay the place off even by retirement age if he wanted to send his son to college. The interest kept growing, and the principal just wouldn't go down. He was floundering in debt as big as the house, and yet he didn't regret buying it.

It was Mr. Y who had suggested the country home when he learned of his situation. Because of the mortgage on the row house, at first he couldn't even imagine moving, and he had absolutely no desire to move to the country. The country house cost so much he would have to transfer the existing mortgage to the buyer of the row house and take out another mortgage that was more than half the original value of the new home. The reason he decided to move despite all this was that Mr. Y had asked him if a house in the country wasn't the ultimate dream of any true city dweller. He thought he should agree if he truly was a city person, so he answered—pounding his chest proudly—"My dream has always been a white single-story house with a pitched roof and a chimney!" After that, he started to believe that living out in the country actually had been a long-cherished dream of his. He hadn't heard Mr. Y muttering under his breath, "Why does everybody think a country house is supposed look like that?" In his mind, he pictured a cloud lightly dancing across a blue sky. Every season, he would plant different flowers in the flower bed in the garden. He would pick lettuce greens and red peppers from the field out back. After he had made the decision to move, he declared to his coworkers that a home in the country was the ultimate dream of any city dweller. Rather than pause in embarrassment at the prepackaged phrases, he bragged that his house was a white single-story home with a pitched roof and a mountain for a backdrop.

*

Even after seeing him hurry into the office, hardly anyone noticed he was late. The man in the next cubicle asked casually, "Did you overdo it last night?" That was it. Everyone was crazy busy with their own work, and the department head would find out about his tardiness only when the weekly timesheets came out. In fact, the morning meeting had been pushed off to the afternoon by the department head, so he used the time to think up some ideas. He came up with a few—all mediocre—but they would have been ignored even if they were good. For important issues, the meetings were usually just a formality, anyway. The important things were decided in advance.

The midday hours flew by. In the end, the meeting was postponed until the following week, so he spent work watching for movement in the stock market. When prices went up, he lamented not having bought any stocks, and when they went down, he bemoaned the weak economy. But there was no way he could own stock. It was just a habit. He chatted at length with the man in the next cubicle about the new city that was advertising for residents. When his coworker said he was seriously considering the solicitation, he mentioned that his own country house was near a planned new city. The coworker showed little interest so he probed, asking if he was tired of living in apartments that were all the same. Even he was surprised by his tone. He had never lived in an apartment.

At quitting time those who had finished their work left one by one, but he stayed because of his tardiness and the backlog he had. He liked staying behind in the office in the city, even when he had no work. He would slowly stroll through the empty office at night. Piles of documents like corpses littering an arena after a battle, conference room chairs strewn about, the large whiteboards with their contents not yet erased, even the coffeemaker with its blinking red light—it looked as though his officemates had left for only a moment, not like they had finished their work and gone home.

Before leaving, he went to the window and surveyed the city. Lights from every building were shining in the night. He liked the cityscape, and he especially enjoyed greeting the night from a building in the heart of downtown. The light from the buildings was beautiful and warm. When he worked late, he particularly liked the fluorescent lights in the building facing his—he could see the people in that building moving busily about. Though it was on the other side of a six-lane street, it was close enough to see clearly into the illuminated offices. He wished he could peer inside with binoculars and find out what business kept people there that late. Even late at night their phones rang off the hook; people were constantly transmitting faxes, feeding paper into a shredder, wearing serious expressions in a meeting; female workers were chitchatting in small groups. He stood at the window watching them and only left in embarrassment when his eyes met someone else's in the building across the way.

The village, which took two hours by highway to reach, was blackness itself. There wasn't a single streetlamp from the highway exit to the new road leading home. The only light on the road was from the headlight beams spewing from the car. He realized again how thick the darkness was in the hills. Whenever he entered the village late at night, the hills lay there like giant dogs and abruptly thrust their shadows out. His only clue was the dogs barking from all directions—only when he heard that sound did he feel the security of having entered the right village. He exited the highway, reached the village by following the barking, found his house by fumbling along the dark new road. The dogs were the only streetlamps and security lights in the village.

When he opened the front door and stepped inside, his wife emerged from behind it, her face pallid. He didn't know why she'd been hiding. He was confused.

"I thought it was them," she said in a shaky voice.

He startled. He realized he had forgotten about them all day. While in the city, he had forgotten he was on the brink of bankruptcy, that marshals would come barging in, that he would have this house taken from him. He hadn't made an effort to forget, nor had he intentionally distracted himself—such things were just naturally forgotten in the city. He received large numbers of business calls, and there was enough work to keep him from thinking about his own finances. Discussing stocks and real estate, he confused bankruptcy and bounty. He might have been less anxious about meeting those marshals if it were in the city. He regretted leaving.

After calming his frightened wife and putting her to bed, he sat quietly in the dark room. He heard what sounded like a machine operating deep underground, so loud he wondered if they had buried the thing while dismantling the factory. Before he knew it, the barking of dogs from the nearby kennels mingled with the mechanical noise from beneath the floor. He mimicked the wailing of the dogs and barked—*woof, woof*—in a low voice. From time to time freight trucks went speeding by like the wind along the highway, and then he could clearly feel the cracks in the new road. Gradually, the house began to seem to him like one huge machine.

*

Several trucks were coming up the new road. His wife grew agitated as soon as she heard the unfamiliar vehicles, and seeing his mother like that, the boy became frightened. The moment he saw the trucks, he too thought the marshals had come. But it could also be new residents moving in. It was a good weekend for moving. The thought of no longer having such peaceful weekends was depressing. His wife grew pale as the trucks neared the house. He decided he would hand the house over without a fight, let the marshals lead him to the chopping block. Rather than cause a scene and let everyone know about the bankruptcy, it was better just to look like they were moving. Six trucks passed by his house bouncing loudly, their cargo compartments full of metal cages stacked high and tight, precarious as though they were on the verge of falling. His wife relaxed her tense features only after hearing them disappear toward the hills.

He wondered if it might be better to leave rather than live in fear, not knowing when the marshals would come. Not that they had a place to go. As he sighed and shook his head, his eyes met those of the man next door. They nodded awkwardly to each other and said hello. Only then did it occur to him that all the home-owners uphill from him were standing in similar poses, watching the trucks. He turned his head and looked downhill. The houses were lined up at regular intervals along the smooth curve of the new road. All the owners of the single-family homes were out-side—either alone or with their families—looking in the direc-tion in which the trucks had disappeared. He was neither shocked nor surprised by this. For him, watching was the only way to show his engagement. The fact that it seemed to be the same for the others gave him a great sense of relief. Though he lived in the country, he was pretty much living the same life as city folk. He waved at the neighbors, who were also used to city life. When he waved, the fourteen households each responded in sequence as if they were doing the wave in a stadium. His lips curled back in a smile—he liked such orderliness. In unison, his neighbors also burst into light, mass-produced laughter.

Once the trucks were gone, his wife brought their son out to the yard with his rubber ball—she seemed relieved. His old mother with Alzheimer's followed them out, naked from the waist down. His wife hurriedly covered her. Moaning, the old woman went back inside, pulled along by the wife's arms. He picked up the hose to water the garden, but the pressure was low and the water barely trickled out. "What a relief," he muttered as he shook water from the hose, not knowing exactly what he meant. Eventually, the marshals would come and totally destroy their normal lives. As he stood there absorbed in thought, the ball rolled up to his foot. He put the hose down and threw the ball to the child. Every time the ball touched his feet, his son burst into laughter, and he laughed along with him.

Their laughter was drowned out by the sound of barking dogs that was so constant it was practically the background noise of the village. This time, though, the sound was more distinct. Several dogs came running down the hill, barking urgently as if being chased by something. You could tell how ferocious they were from their barking. At the sudden dog noises, the child clung to the fence. He told him to go inside because these dogs were vicious. That was obvious once they'd reached the new road—they had distinct bald patches, clumps of fur missing because of mange. None of the village homes had a dog. These must have been from the kennels. He muttered all of a sudden, "The kennels must be just over the hill." But in the past, the barking had come from all sides; he couldn't really be sure where the kennels were.

His son threw the ball out of the yard. It skittered down the new road, and in a flash, he had climbed over the fence to retrieve it. Startled, he ran after the boy, but the dogs reached his son before he did. They completely surrounded the child, drove their ferocious teeth into him. He tried to stay calm, but his body shook and his legs wouldn't move. He looked around for a weapon to hit the dogs with. Nothing caught his eye. He grabbed whatever he could; he threw the pebbles that were strewn over the yard, but no matter how many times he hit them, they weren't hurt. In desperation, he yelled at them. His wife came running out, alarmed by the screaming, and his mother came running naked behind her. The dogs refused to let go of the boy. His wife went back inside and came out with a long-handled broom and his son's baseball bat. It was a light aluminum bat—he swung it wildly at the dogs, yelling for the neighbors at the same time. There was no one to help. They must have gone inside when they heard the dogs, locking their doors tight. He should have taken the boy and gone inside, too. He regretted not doing that. In the distance, hundreds of dogs were barking at once, as if chastising him for his negligence. The growls of the dogs tearing at the boy mingled with the cries of the dogs howling in the distance. *Why were the dogs at the kennels crying out so much today?* he thought as he swung the bat, feeling like he wanted to weep. He swung blindly—he couldn't even tell if it was a dog or his son he was hitting with the bat. The dogs bit and tore at the boy until they were exhausted, then slowly trotted down the new road.

The boy lay still, the flesh torn on his chest and arms. The dog bites swelled up red. When she saw the state he was in, his wife burst into tears. He told his wife—who was screaming and crying uncontrollably—to bring a blanket; he wrapped the boy in it and carefully placed him in the car. His old mother hurriedly climbed in, not even properly dressed.

He couldn't figure out where the hospital was. He just followed the new road down to the village entrance. The man who owned house #6 was outside watering his garden. He asked the way to the nearest hospital. The man put down the hose and shouted excitedly that it was in the direction of the kennels, raising his hand to point toward the hills. He turned the car around and drove back up toward the hills. Just to be safe, he also asked the man from #17—who was out in his yard pulling weeds—where the hospital was. The man also quickly replied that he had heard

41

there was a hospital in the direction of the kennels. From the urgent tone of their voices, he knew the neighbors had watched his child getting hurt. He gave a half-hearted thanks and sped away. The boy's moaning was quieter. He was afraid that meant he was getting weaker. He wanted to make the boy scream, even if he had to hit him. His wife—cradling the child—kept crying. He couldn't concentrate on finding his way because of the crying. He had never gone toward the kennels before. To go there, he had to get his bearings by listening for the barking dogs. He told his wife to be quiet. She sniffled and swallowed her tears.

Before he knew it, they were halfway up the hill. The new road connected to up there. He stopped the car. The dogs stopped barking. He started again. The dogs started barking again. He couldn't tell whether it was the dogs' barking or phantom noises made by his ears. "Honey, do you hear the dogs barking?" he asked his wife. He couldn't stand it, the savage growling around his ears. "What are you talking about, just go!" his wife yelled, choking back tears. Quickly, he started driving again, wanting to cry himself. They crested the hill, awash in the sound of the dogs' barking. A development just like their own village appeared on the other side. He was afraid he might be driving in circles. It was exactly like their village: pure white metal-framed single-story homes all lined up and precisely spaced like dominoes. It looked like, if you pushed over the last house, the whole complex would come tumbling down. The new road continued to the end of the village.

He stopped the car and asked a man who was out in his yard where the nearest hospital was. The man was watering his flower bed; he put down the hose he was holding. "If you go toward the kennels, there is a large hospital," he said. He asked the man where the kennels were, and the man looked around in all directions, confused. There weren't just one or two kennels, the man said. He'd heard they were over the hill. He pointed in the direction they had come. "It's over that hill," he said. "I heard dogs barking in that direction." He sighed in despair. He thought maybe he was better off relying on the dogs' barking. The boy was breathing quietly as if he were asleep, and his wife's crying had changed to sobs. He wanted to cry like his wife. Anger welled up, but the tears wouldn't come.

He went on without thinking, just following the sound. The dogs were barking more ferociously than ever. They were barking from all directions. When he went north, he wondered if the kennels might be to the south, and when he turned right, he wondered if he shouldn't have turned left. He turned the wheel whichever way his arms moved. Sometimes the barking seemed to get closer, and sometimes it faded away. If it weren't for the boy, he would have gone to the kennels first. The dogs that tore his son's flesh were surely being raised at the kennels. He wanted to beat the dogs in their cages. But what if they weren't from the kennels? They might have been stray dogs you could find wandering in any village, strays that might be even more vicious than dogs from a kennel. He became confused—was he looking for the kennels, a hospital for treating his son, or the dogs that bit him?

On his way down the new road, he unwittingly entered the highway and had to keep going. Could the kennels have been toward that hill? He regretted driving straight over the hill and not searching other roads while he was on it. If he had gotten off the new road and gone deeper into the hills, he might have been able to locate the kennels. Before he could dwell on his mistake, he heard the barking again. The noise sounded diffuse enough for the entire city to seem like a kennel. It sounded loud, like it was close, but with the wind beating against the windshield, he still couldn't guess the direction.

The truck behind him changed lanes and sped ahead, followed by another truck rumbling past. Though usually he never went over the speed limit on the highway, he decided to tail them. To get the boy to the hospital quickly, it was best to follow the trucks. Luckily, he could still hear the barking. He casually glanced up at the tailgate of the truck he was following and was stunned. The cargo bed was stacked precariously high with cages, and in each one was a dog. All the while, the dogs were looking down at his car and barking as he drove. His old mother's eyes grew wide; her body trembled in fear. His wife burst into tears again as she bundled the boy tightly in the blanket. The boy's breathing was still shallow. Following the truck with the barking dogs, exceeding the speed limit, he looked behind him again and again. He had no idea if he was going in the right direction, toward the kennels. Behind were only cars chasing him—speeding, seeming to threaten him like the dogs that bit his son. Darkness was quickly catching up with the cars.

Chasing after the truck, he was soon at the tollgates at the entrance to the city. He could see it beyond the gates—drowned in pitch darkness, without a single light. A female attendant with an expressionless face handed him a ticket. The name of the city he worked in was printed on it, but the lightless city he saw was unfamiliar, and he wasn't sure if he was entering the city or his village. He couldn't see the truck anymore, but the barking guided him like streetlights. He picked up speed, following the sound that would lead him to the kennels. The road would end eventually. If he kept following it to the end, he would reach someplace. He thought it would be good if they were headed toward the kennels.

—Translated by Yoosup Chang and Heinz Insu Fenkl

BIRTH OF THE ZOO

A Siberian wolf had gone missing. A beast forty-seven inches long, with a nineteen-inch-long tail and weighing 103 pounds. Or maybe even bigger, and heavier. The reported measurements were a month old, from when the animals had their last regular checkups.

The missing wolf had been fond of climbing onto a low boulder and staring off into the distance, its legs so much longer and stronger than those of the other wolves. Its body would form a smooth line from its perked-up ears all the way down to its tail. It was hard to tell just what it was looking at with those deep golden eyes. Its appetite was ferocious. Unsatisfied by the two plucked and cleaned chickens it was given each mealtime, it spent the rest of the day chewing on sticks. According to the experts, a wolf could go five days without eating. They never said what would happen after those five days.

"It will turn up in residential areas first," the experts said worriedly. "And it will attack whatever it sees."

The looks in their eyes made it easy to understand what they meant by "whatever."

A little farther up the slope past the wolf's cage were the enclosures for other large predators like tigers and lions. Their enclosures contained small springs, shade trees, and large boulders where they could stretch out and rest. Compared to the wolf's cage, which was surrounded by a tightly woven wire fence and lacked even a single tuft of grass, the big cat enclosures might as well have been actual savanna. The cramped dimensions of the wolf's cage showed just how unpopular it was with zoo guests. Besides, Siberian wolves weren't even endangered. At midday, or peak zoo attendance, the wolf was usually napping. When it finally awoke, it would stare at onlookers with lifeless eyes. Zoo guests quickly grew bored and walked away from a wolf that didn't so much as sniff around or tear apart raw meat with its sharp fangs or growl threateningly at them and so they would move on to the next attraction. To them, the wolf was nothing special, just one among many animals living in a zoo.

Its disappearance wasn't discovered until late in the afternoon. An inner door used only by the zookeeper had been left open. Because the door was unlocked from the outside, it was assumed the wolf had been stolen rather than escaped on its own. No one knew how anyone could possibly have gotten out of the zoo with a wolf in tow. That day, the zookeeper had taken longer than usual to do his rounds. He had skipped feeding the wolf entirely, the investigation revealed, which was why it took so long for anyone to realize its cage was empty. Until the news reports came out, zoo guests had strolled right past the cage, oblivious to the occupant's absence. The zookeeper was fired. People marveled over the golden eyes of the wolf that made the news. By disappearing, it finally became popular.

A few days later the aviary was damaged. The aviary was in the shape of a dome whose highest point was a good sixteen feet off the ground. The tight metal bars in the roof had been bent outward. There had been a violent storm off the coast that day. The city's anemometers had worked harder than usual. Signs had been downed, structures had blown over, pedestrians were injured. But the only thing to lose its roof was the aviary, home to a single species of bird. The birds had escaped through the hole torn in the roof. Ash-gray feathers were found on the ground. The zoo fretted about not knowing exactly how many birds were on the loose, for their records didn't match the zookeepers' estimates. The locals couldn't care less about the number of lost birds. If anything, they watched the news with amusement. Compared to a wolf, birds were nothing to be afraid of. But the zoo authorities *were* afraid. First a wolf had vanished, and then a flock of birds had flown off. For all they knew, it was a prank to make the zoo look bad. Sure enough, the zoo's image did suffer. Officials decided to close the zoo temporarily under the pretext of repairs. Really, it was to improve security. Their plan was to install security cameras in every single animal enclosure.

Immediately after the zoo made the decision to close, gunshots began to ring out across the city.

*

The man turned toward the sound of gunfire. In the darkness, the buildings were slowly revealing themselves. Sound scattered as it traveled through the frigid night air, making it hard to tell exactly where it had come from. He let out a long exhale. His breath turned white. He saw where his breath vanished and slowly walked in that direction. It led him to a low hill tucked among the buildings. At the top was a small, octagonal pavilion. That seemed to be where the gunshot had come from. Clad only in slippers, his feet ached from the cold. The temperature was dropping. He had heard the gun and rushed out. The wolf would soon be facing a cold snap. He wondered which would kill it first: cold or starvation.

He was about to climb the hill when another shot rang out. The sound echoed across the sky like thunder. At the same time a lightning bolt flashed across his mind. The gunfire had sounded close, but like before it was difficult to track where it was coming from. The untraceable gunshots would continue all night, as they had every night before.

He'd wet himself the first time he heard a gunshot. It had sounded so close he thought the person standing next to him was hit. The next time, he felt like the bullet had lodged in his own heart. He could practically hear the blood spurting from his chest. As he'd roamed the city in pursuit of the wolf, he stopped fearing the sound of gunfire. Instead, he grew fond of the quiet stillness that followed the long, loud rifle shots.

Everyone was in agreement that the wolf needed to be stopped. The wolf was a threat. A corpse had been found—it was assumed the person had been mauled to death by the wolf. The corpse was hideous. Every part that could be bitten had been chewed on. It lay sprawled out on the asphalt with its intestines ripped out. Of course, there was no way to be sure it was the wolf's doing. Not so much as a single strand of wolf fur had been found in the dried, clotted blood. There were no bloody paw prints. The only certainty was that the person had been bitten by something sharp.

Very few people had actually seen the body, and yet rumors spread like wildfire. One of the rumors was that part of the body was missing. This was followed by speculation that the hungry wolf had eaten the missing body part. The news reported that wolves' strong teeth were capable of tearing and mashing and could therefore easily sever the limbs of a mammal no matter the size. They claimed a wolf's teeth could pulverize the strongest of bones. It was imperative that the wolf be put down as quickly as possible; its vicious, repugnant image was proof.

Yet, dead person or no, the police couldn't spend all their time chasing a wolf. The city had plenty of problems aside from a missing predator. The administration invoked the Pest Control Law, which gave official permission for anyone to kill any birds or other animals causing harm to crops or human beings. The wolf was classified as a pest. After the law took effect, gun sales went through the roof. Gunfire began to ring out across the city. The police turned a blind eye to it all, ignoring complaints from citizens startled by the sound of gunfire or simply not investigating reports of gun activity. They washed their hands of anything to do with the wolf.

A black shadow slept curled up beneath the pavilion. He cautiously approached the shadow. It was a large person dressed in animal skins. The person in furs didn't react to his approach. He sank down next to him.

Already several days had passed since the man had begun wandering the city in search of the wolf. There was no question the wolf was still in the city. The incessant sound of gunfire was proof of that. But despite the ongoing gunfire, he had yet to see so much as a single wolf hair. Witnesses kept coming forth, saying they'd spotted the wolf, but it was impossible to confirm whether what they saw was actually a wolf or just a dog that looked like a wolf. As the wolf's whereabouts grew less certain, talk began to circulate that maybe it had never escaped in the first place. Maybe the negligent zookeeper had made it all up rather than admit that a wolf had sickened and died on his watch. It wasn't as if the wolf could have opened its cage door and strolled away. The wolf hunters didn't believe this story. They believed there was a wolf lurking in the city somewhere.

The person in furs awoke and held out his hand to the man.

"If you've got any smokes, could I have one?"

He offered the person a cigarette.

"What's with the rifle?" the person asked.

He stroked the barrel of the gun and said, "It's for the wolf."

The person nodded.

"This city is full of wolf hunters."

As if in response, a shot rang out somewhere.

"Sounds just like fireworks, don't it?" the person said. "The sound, I mean."

He smirked in lieu of agreement. If it were only fireworks, there'd be no danger of people dying gruesome deaths. The rifle muzzles swung around in search of a wolf, but all that died were the abandoned dogs that roamed the city. The hunters shot at every animal they encountered in the city at night.

"Every time I hear that sound, I expect to see a rainbow of fireworks," the man said, stubbing out his cigarette. "Instead all I see are bleeding dogs."

The person in furs dropped low to the ground like a four-legged animal. His body was covered from head to toe in animal skins.

The man laughed out loud as he watched the person pull a fur hood down over his face with one hand.

"What on earth are you doing?"

"Check me out. I'm a wolf."

The fur person waved at him, let out a howl, and crawled down the hill.

"Your ass is too high! And you've got no tail," the man yelled loudly after him. Mouthing the word "bang," he pretended to aim his rifle at the person, who slowly vanished down the hill. A tail-less wolf in dirty furs. Ha. The only thing the wolf and the person in furs had in common was that they were both male.

There were many others as well who'd covered themselves in animal skins. Coats modeled after the wolf's own coat had grown popular. Men purchased these coats and not necessarily because of the bitter weather about to befall them. Wolf masks were a popular item among children. Children in plastic wolf masks could be seen on every street. The masked children howled at the sky like wolves. Toy cars and bicycles adorned with wolf figures appeared in shops. There was even a coin-operated wolf train. When you inserted a coin, the train let out a howl and lurched forward again and again for five minutes with a child on board. Some children wore bird wings instead. They used rubber bands to attach the long wings to their arms and leapt from high places. The wings were useless for creating lift. The children fell; limbs were injured.

As time passed, the birds came to be feared more than the man-eating wolf. That was because they appeared during the day, too. They let out low, unpleasant cries and formed a large flock that cast dark shadows everywhere they went. They shat everywhere and pecked at everything they could. They pecked at a baby in a stroller when the parents' backs were turned. They pecked at the legs of an elderly person who already had trouble walking and caused them to trip and fall. A rumor went around that a vulture had escaped from the zoo and eaten a corpse. This meant the body had been lying in the street long enough to be picked clean by vultures, which made people angry at the police.

People panicked at the sight of birds. Birds flocked to airports, disrupting flight paths. This had always been a problem at airports, but everyone blamed the birds from the zoo. They planted feed laced with poison around the city. Innocent homeless people died. The birds shat on the bodies of the dead homeless.

People gathered to talk about the missing animals. But only during the day. Once night fell, they rushed to lock their doors. The city after dark belonged to the birds that flew low in search of prey and the hunters in search of a wolf. There was only one wolf, but there were countless hunters. It was terrifying to bump into one of them in an out-of-the-way alley without even a single security light. Most carried unlicensed firearms. The rumors kept coming of people gunned down by hunters. A bullet could pass right through a heart without anyone knowing who the bullet belonged to.

No reports came of the wolf's capture. Maybe it had already been captured. The activity in the black market was more telling than the press. And even if the wolf were caught, the hunters were not about to let the press know. If they did, they would have to hand over their precious prey for just a small sum and nothing else to show for their labor. A reward wasn't what those who rushed out to hunt every night wanted. For city people who had never encountered anything that could be described as wild, an escaped wolf—and most still believed that the wolf and the birds had escaped from the zoo—was the wildest and most attractive thing there was.

He, too, wandered every corner of the city in search of the wolf. He would plan his route according to other people's sightings. Most happened downtown. Some said they saw the wolf in front of the entrance to a large department store; others, in a high-rise apartment complex. He believed them all. Because he, too, had seen the wolf in the heart of the city.

He had gotten very, very drunk that night. His coworkers, who were all similarly inebriated, staggered out to the curb to catch taxis. He waved them goodbye and stumbled down the sidewalk. The shadows of familiar skyscrapers fell darkly upon him. He found himself heading toward the subway, though the trains would have stopped running by then. He marveled at how his legs remembered his habits. He was used to taking the subway whenever possible, even very late at night, to save on cab fare. To catch a cab going in the right direction, he had to cross the street, which was empty. It was unusual for there to be no cars at all even in the dead of night. There must have been a whole line of them somewhere waiting for a green light.

He was halfway across the street, checking to make sure no cars were coming, when he saw the wolf. It was heading toward him. All at once the street turned silent; he felt like he'd stepped into a vacuum. Figuring he was even drunker than he'd thought, he stopped dead in the middle. His body swayed slowly in the direction of the earth's rotation.

The wolf loped toward him. He didn't know if it was the

moonlight or starlight or the headlights of distant cars, but a strange radiance illuminated the wolf. Its body gave off a silvery glow. Its slanted, golden eyes glared gently at him. When his eyes met the wolf's, something stirred in him. That was how it felt anyway, though nothing actually changed. Except the alcohol that had filled his body to the crown of his head evaporated all at once. As he stood there staring, the wolf passed by him and slowly disappeared into the city. He remained rooted in place, gazing after the wolf that was already long gone.

He worked for an insurance company. The bulk of his paycheck went to his elderly mother in the countryside. She had slipped on a snowy road the winter before and cracked her hip, leaving her bedridden. Despite the money he sent her, it was unlikely she ever went to the hospital. She lived more than five hours away from him. He rarely made the trip except for holidays, and sometimes not even then, as he'd claim to be too busy. With only the two of them left to remember departed family members, the memorial table was nearly bare, and lonely. He never ate breakfast, and for dinner he got by on bar snacks or simple things from the nearby *kimbap* place. He stayed late at the office most nights due to his workload and went in most weekends as well. It was hard to make time to see friends. And yet, because he was somehow always behind, his performance reviews always faulted him for working too slowly. Now and then he wondered if working late and on weekends wasn't in fact the reason for his bad performance reviews, but he was so behind on his work that he had no choice but to keep staying late and coming in on weekends. He spent his days off catching up on laundry. His old machine had a leaky hose; each spin cycle flooded his kitchen floor. The drain in the floor was always backed up, too. After the laundry was done, the water would remain pooled on the floor for more than two days. He stood in the soapy water and hung his wash from a line strung across the kitchen. Laundry day always turned his half-basement flat into a damp, weeping mess. Black-and-blue mold bloomed across the ceiling and walls. He spent the remainder of his day off tracing images of the wolf he'd seen the night before in the patterns formed by the mold.

Despite the fact that he had nothing else to do, time flew and another Monday morning saw him off to work without breakfast. He loped along slowly, imitating the wolf's stride. Always the last to show up for work and often late to boot, he arrived late again that day. Everyone, including his manager, turned in unison to stare as he came through the door. The office fell silent. On any other day he would have thought the way they looked at him—some staring, others pretending not to stare—meant someone had been speaking ill of him. His team had been busy with a new project. He was hard-pressed to keep up. The other team members had all worked through the weekend. His footsteps rang out in the quiet office. He listened to the sound of his own shoes peeling off of the linoleum and thought about the wolf. The wolf that had slowly crossed the street and disappeared into a darkened alleyway. The wolf had looked up at him with those soft eyes, its brow lowered.

He made his eyes like the wolf's and went over to his manager.

"Were you sick yesterday?" his manager asked gently. "Everyone else showed up."

He shook his head.

"I wasn't sick."

"Then what was it?" Now his manager sounded irritated. "You weren't sick, but you still took the whole weekend off and came in late?"

"It was the wolf."

The manager said loudly, "What?" as if he hadn't heard him. When he just stood there, the manager twirled his pen at him to hurry him up. While being reprimanded, he kept looking up at the manager from beneath his brow. He couldn't force the wolf to close those golden eyes. With his brow lowered, he told his manager he quit.

"What're you going to do now?" The manager's tone had softened slightly.

"I'm going to find the wolf."

The manager had nothing to say to that but merely stared for a moment before ordering an underling to fetch a resignation form.

One of his coworkers tried to dissuade him by saying that he was wasting his time: "Not like you have to go far to find a wolf. The world is full of them."

He imagined lowering his brow at the coworker. The coworker looked at his closed eyes in confusion.

*

Now and then he thought about what it was that had him so entranced. Was it the kindness that he saw in the wolf's golden eyes, the soft pelt that would fetch a nice price, or the meat that was bound to be stringy but exotic? He had no idea.

He tightened his grip on the gun. He'd never fired one before.

It was loaded with seven bullets. If the wolf appeared, he would have to end its life in seven shots.

At first he'd gone after the wolf empty-handed.

"What're you gonna do? Knock it out with your fists?" someone blurted out at him.

He'd seen this person before in other parts of the city. The person always carried a long rifle on his shoulder.

He saw his first real-life gun while on his wolf hunt. The only thought in his head was that he had to find the wolf again; it hadn't occurred to him that he should probably be armed. The only thing he knew about guns was that you had to keep them locked up at the police station.

The person showed him where to buy a gun. He went along, despite wondering if the person was running some kind of scam. Or maybe the person wasn't even a wolf hunter himself but a gun smuggler preying on wannabe wolf hunters. He stared at the person's rifle and then down at his own clenched fists. His hands, used only for tapping away at an electronic calculator to determine insurance premiums, were smooth and pale. They didn't look like they could kill a cockroach, let alone a wolf. For hunting in the city, a gun was a necessity. Supposedly, in some parts of Africa, it was customary to spend the night alone in the bush before learning to hunt. To be a hunter, you had to know how to read the direction of the wind, imitate animal sounds, find water. He'd never stayed up all night alone in the city and didn't know the first thing about reading the wind or using the stars to orient himself. Since he couldn't do any of those things, he figured, at the very least he ought to have a gun.

The person led him along a winding route through narrow,

dirty alleys that all looked the same. Maybe this convoluted path had been purposely chosen to make it impossible for him to find his way back on his own. He lost count of how many dark, cramped, foul-smelling back alleys they wandered down before finally arriving at a dilapidated, unmarked cigarette shop. Inside, a small group of men was playing cards. They didn't look happy to see him. The person gave one of the men a look; he lifted a blind concealing the back of the shop, slipped inside, and returned with an old rifle.

The barrel looked rough and shoddy, so he chose his words carefully.

"Does it fire?"

The men in the store all laughed.

"If it doesn't fire, is it still a gun?"

He peered into the long, dark muzzle of the gun. He thought he could hear an animal cry out somewhere.

The person took the rifle from him and led him to a shooting range. Live-fire shooting ranges had become wildly popular ever since the wolf had gone missing. The person told him that back in his college days he'd medaled in a national marksmanship competition. As befitting someone who'd once been nationally ranked, the former marksman hit all of the targets well. The man pulled the trigger the way the marksman taught him. The bullet flew off somewhere into the back of the shooting range.

Pulling the trigger for the first time gave him a peculiar feeling. The bullet exploding out of the barrel seemed to mark an end to his old life. He had to kill the wolf, he just had to. Finally, he had an aim in life.

*

There it was. Behind the building's vent. Its enormous black shadow was slinking around. Taking care not to make a sound, he crept closer to the shadow. The former marksman, who'd turned up again out of nowhere, followed quietly. Hunters were always crossing paths after dark. The shadow was slowly moving. As he drew nearer, his hands became moist. The shadow rested its large body on the pavement. He swallowed. The sound of him swallowing echoed through the city.

Somewhere a bird called. Several birds were circling in the night sky. If not for their cackling cries, he wouldn't have known they were birds. Birds flying in flocks looked like dark clouds. He ran his eyes over the shadow. It was still curled up there on the ground, indifferent to anything as trivial as birdsong. He slipped off his shoes to muffle his footsteps. Smears of discarded food stuck to his bare feet.

The beast had its back to him with its tail upraised. He inched toward it. The closer he got, the clearer the outlines of the shadow. He could practically feel the rough fur that covered its body. He wiped the sweat from his hands onto his pants. The other man already had his gun trained on the wolf. It made him anxious that the former marksman might fire first. But then again, he was probably better able to subdue the wolf without killing it. A bullet from his own gun might either miss the wolf entirely or kill it. The thought made his hands shake. He had to fire now or he would lose the wolf forever. Crossing paths with a wolf twice was no easy feat. He thought about how he'd trembled the first time he fired a gun at the shooting range. The quake that passed through him when the bullet left the gun, the roar that threatened to rend his eardrums, the recoil that left him shaking. He aimed his rifle with great care and stilled his breath in preparation for squeezing the trigger.

Gunfire echoed long and loud through the forest of tall buildings. No sooner was he thinking about letting out a big exhale than the bullet was in flight. Unlike his mind, his body had been unfazed. The time that had elapsed between him spotting the wolf and firing the gun felt longer than his whole life up to that moment. That single bullet seemed to pierce the entire length of his life. The shadow shivered and coughed. The smell of gunpowder stung his nose. The former marksman approached the fallen shadow and fired another shot into it. The shadow coughed and shivered again. Dark blood ran down the pavement. It reached his bare feet. His feet grew wet. The bullet had pierced the body of the black shadow. That was when he realized what he'd been hoping for wasn't the death of a wolf.

What lay on the ground was a man dressed head to toe in animal skins. He remembered him. It was the same man who'd been dressed like a wolf and crawled downhill on all fours. Or maybe it wasn't. There were a great many people in the streets dressed in furs. The skins they wore were so similar that they all looked alike.

The fallen man gazed up at him, his eyes blinking weakly. He sank to the ground. The wounded man's stomach rose and fell, and each time it did, blood poured from his torn belly. The marksman sank down too, looking shocked. He rummaged in his pockets and pulled out a juice box of alcohol. He tore it open with his teeth and took a big swig. Then he offered it to him. The marksman's hand shook. He silently accepted the alcohol. Now and then, the man on the ground shivered as if life was clinging hard to him. His breathing grew quieter. Maybe it wasn't *his* gun that had shot the man. Just because he was still warm didn't necessarily mean his injuries were fresh.

The former marksman reached into another pocket and pulled out a handful of shredded dried squid. It was hard. It took great effort to chew and swallow. The shadow on the ground would pant occasionally as if in pain. Each time that happened, he took another swig of alcohol and held it in his mouth. The towering buildings cast cold shadows on their shoulders. He slowly lifted his head, his eyes tracing their shadows. But no matter how far back he leaned his head, he couldn't make out the night sky hidden behind the buildings. He felt like he was inside a tall, domed concrete cage. The birds circling in the air looked down at them like prison guards.

He moved closer to the bleeding man and stroked the bloody fur. It was softer than he'd expected. The birds flew lower and cried out. Maybe they were vultures, alert to the fact of someone dying. They circled night and day. Their enormous wings cast uncanny shadows everywhere. When night fell, they sought out the shadowy places between buildings, tucked their beaks, and folded their wings.

Gunfire rang out again somewhere close. The building's shadow trembled in its wake. The birds stilled their cries, as if they, too, were startled.

"You figure there's something over there?" the marksman said, gazing into the dark.

"Maybe," the man said, his voice trembling. "Maybe it's the wolf."

"Then we should probably head over there, too, no?"

The marksman stood and brushed off his pants. He stood, too. The fur-covered man lay quietly as if asleep. His blood spread like a blanket thrown across the road. They stuffed what was left of the dried squid into their mouths. It was more than they could chew. Saliva spilled from their lips with each bite. Without bothering to wipe the drool from his face, he went toward the sound of the gunfire. With each step, the blood on the pavement stuck to his feet. He pulled the hems of his pants up and wiped his bare soles. The air, which had grown terribly cold, chilled his feet. He hurried, limping as he went.

*

At the bus stop stood a long line of students in school uniforms. He got in line with them, clutching his aching stomach. His back had been damp with sweat all morning. His new job was at another insurance company. Sales this time. The company dress code forbade him from wearing short sleeves even in summer.

Whenever he happened to walk down one of the city's back alleys, he would taste again that tough dried squid and feel something clinging to the soles of his feet. The alleys were littered with foul-smelling bags of garbage. Cats and pigeons and flies prowled, fleeing when he drew near. He never found any bloodstains on the pavement. Nor could he remember where exactly the fur-covered man had lain. The city had a great many back alleys that were dark with shadows and patrolled by feral cats chasing the stink of garbage.

Gunfire still rang out now and then in the city. Though he was never really sure if it was random gunfire or a gun salute to mark some festival. There were a lot of festivals, and they were always accompanied by fireworks and gun salutes.

He checked his watch anxiously. If the bus didn't come soon, he would be late again. He opened a newspaper to try to calm his nerves. He scanned the paper carefully every single day, but there was never any mention of the dead man. Maybe that kind of death was commonplace. Above the newspaper, a dark shadow wavered. It was a bird. A single black bird had been following him ever since he'd left home that morning. Each time he turned to look up, it flew higher and circled. The large bird resembled a vulture. He had no idea why a carrion-eating bird would keep following him.

Wolf sightings had continued. At one point, nine people in five different locations claimed to have seen the wolf. All of them were at an apartment complex near the zoo. As if out for a stroll, the wolf had walked leisurely from building to building, sniffed at some bags of food compost, and rummaged through them. It tore open some of the bags and ate from them. Those who saw the wolf thought it was a stray dog and kicked at it to chase it off. Some of the children had been bitten by dogs before. As the economy had worsened, the number of abandoned dogs and cats had grown. The abandoned animals varied in size and kind but were alike in the fact that they had all grown filthy and disheveled.

When the bus finally arrived, the man squeezed his body on board like a piece of luggage. If traffic wasn't too bad on the way to the subway station, he might avoid being late. This coming weekend, he would have to head down to his mother's house in the country. She had been calling him constantly to ask if he was okay, saying she was having terrible dreams. The thought of the trouble his bedridden mother had to go to just to call weighed on him. He told her each time that everything was fine. And everything *was* fine. His flat still flooded—the floor brimming with tears—and bloomed with mildew whenever he did the laundry. Every morning he still eyed his watch nervously for fear of being late even though he always skipped breakfast. He was still swamped at work and spent his free days at the office. And though he would stagger drunk across the street, he suffered no accidents.

There was one other person besides his elderly mother who would ask how he was doing. This was the former marksman. He would call and ask the man if he didn't want to join him for another nighttime hunt. When the man refused, the marksman would say, "Do you know when the hunt is over for the hunter?"

The man would start to say, "When the hunter is dead," but was always too annoyed to get the words out.

"When the prey has been caught," the marksman would say. "That's when it's over."

The man would retort that he'd never once considered himself a hunter. The marksman always scoffed at that.

The man got off the bus and hurried to the subway entrance. He could hear a bird crying. He looked up at the sky. There was no sign of the bird that had been following him. As he stood there looking up and blocking the entrance, someone bumped into him. He moved aside to clear the way and stepped on a lump of something. It stuck to the sole of his shoe. Whatever it was made it difficult to walk. He limped down the stairs. Halfway down, he paused to try scraping the sole of his shoe against the edge of the step, but no matter how much he rubbed, it wouldn't come unstuck. He teetered on one leg to examine the sole. The inner edge of the heel was worn down, but other than that, there was nothing there. If he wanted to get to work on time, he couldn't dally any longer. He ran the rest of the way, half-limping as he went.

—Translated by Sora Kim-Russell

NIGHT WORK

The damaged wall was bordered by a thicket of prickly hogweed and densely leaved trees that sheltered a marshy pond. The vegetation was so overgrown, with branches going every which way, it hid the marsh from view. It also helped conceal the wall, which resembled a sheet of paper with its corner folded. Since the thicket wasn't on the same side as the burial mound, passersby never noticed it.

The house was at the end of an alley that resembled a narrow colonnade, with the burial mound in back and the thicket to its right. No one knew who the burial mound belonged to or how old it was. What was clear was that it had been there since before D City was designated a city and before the country came to be called by its current name. D City had far too many of these ancient burial mounds. So many that not even the Cultural Heritage Administration could investigate every one of them. Most were left unattended with only some barbed wire fencing thrown up around them, and whoever's body and whatever burial goods they contained remained an enduring mystery. Which grave might belong to an ancient king and which to the traitor who'd plotted the king's death was anyone's guess.

The surface of the marsh was choked with watershield, water thyme, and other aquatic plants that made it impossible to gauge the depth. From higher up, it resembled a well-tended lawn. A little lower, and it looked just like a freshly paved road. Most of the watershield and water thyme were blackened and long dead, floating rootlessly, filling the pond with a mushy, mucusy mass so uninviting it might as well have been concrete. Not even the wind seemed capable of stirring its surface, yet it did sometimes ripple. Such as when his wife caught a field mouse inside the house and swung it around by the tail before flinging it into the pond, or when the village sewage pipe released its filth into it. The marsh would slosh briefly to acknowledge it had received everything. At those times, the bottomless bog would reveal its pitch-black insides. The dark, dirty dregs, the untold depths, the putrid hole. He stayed as far away from it as possible.

Back when his wife had told him the house came with a pond, he'd pictured a dainty green frog perched atop a glistening lily pad. Indeed, the water was covered in padlike leaves floating on the surface, but they were as filthy as their tangled mess of stems. The slime surrounding them was cloudy and thick like expelled phlegm. It was no place for small green frogs. Instead, what frequented the pond were enormous bullfrogs that croaked at all hours of the day and night, rodents that preyed on the bullfrogs, cats that preyed on the rodents, and enormous feral cats stalking the much smaller house cats. Every loud, dirty thing seemed to gather at the marsh.

Rumors about the marsh ran wild in the village. One was that a young woman had drowned in it. The rumor was so old there was no telling whether there was any truth to it. Everyone said it was pointless to dredge the water for her corpse, since her white bones would have turned to mud by then. Another rumor was that, after she drowned, the young men of the village began to disappear one by one. Of course, they were probably lost not to the pond but to the city. What really kept the villagers away was the smell—the reek of wet, rotting leaves and stagnant water. It stank of sunken dead rodents, feral cats, and, as rumor had it, people. Worse, the sewer pipe that ran through the neighborhood terminated at the marsh. Excrement, food scraps, and dead pets flowed through it to no end. Everything discarded collected in the pond.

The smell carried as far as the entrance to the village. It nauseated the sensitive and newcomers alike. It brought to mind dead bodies moldering under a scorching sun.

"What kind of shameless idiot bathes a corpse at home in this weather?"

That was his wife's reaction when, standing before the gaping front door of the house, she first encountered the smell. Her parents had died instantly in a traffic accident on their way to meet their newborn grandchild, and she had to hold their funeral while still recovering from giving birth. Their house passed down to her. The little square house, which tilted slightly to one side, had two rooms, a narrow veranda, a semi-detached kitchen, and a cracked garden wall. The crack had grown over the years and was reaching toward where the wall connected with the house. If this continued, it would split their inner quarters in two.

More offensive than the smell were the rodents. The family's noses soon grew accustomed to the smells; they breathed, ate, and yawned the unrelenting stench. But rodents were impossible to get used to. The mice and rats feared nothing. Now and then a feral cat would appear and they'd scatter with their tails between their legs, but after a moment they'd return in droves and attack the cat. Living here had taught him their unusual capacity for aggression. Sometimes, the rodents and feral cats even slunk around the garden together like companions. He never saw any house mice. What lurked in the kitchen and under the veranda were wild ratlike creatures with sharp teeth and long, black fur. They were a much bigger pest than feral cats. Cats at least caught mice, but rats were good for absolutely nothing. With breeding season lasting till mid-May, the rodents beneath the garden wall would squeal and chatter as they birthed baby after baby well into the approach of winter. They dug holes for nests for their dozens of squirming, hairless pink pups under the cracked wall. If he didn't fill in the crack or just knock the whole wall down, they would slowly creep closer and closer until they reached the house.

Their child brought one of the babies inside and tried to raise it as a pet. They had no idea what she'd done until she screamed one day and burst into tears, her ear bitten by the rodent, which had grown larger than her own fat forearm. It sprang from under her bedding. It was the biggest, dirtiest, smelliest creature he'd ever seen. Timid as he was, he fainted, and the animal ran back and forth over his chest in its attempts to escape. The child ran around the tiny room chasing after it. His wife used her spoon to corner it. When they shook out the bedding, black droppings flew everywhere. For all he knew, they'd been breathing in its feces and dried saliva. For days afterward, he was plagued by a high fever, and even after the fever broke he kept taking fever reducers. He burned the soiled bedding and clothing in the garden. Black smoke covered the house like a roof. No one in the village asked what the smoke was from. It lingered over their house before disappearing over the marsh. His wife had tossed the squirming rodent into the burning blanket. It raced back into the house, its body in flames, while he and his wife chased after it with water bottles.

The whole year round, the constant whine of insects was so loud it made their ears ache. Swarms of mosquitoes buzzed the rims of their ears all the way into winter. Crickets, katydids, and cicadas started their moaning in the early spring. By then, the dragonflies had already laid their eggs. The ground around the garden tap was white with them. Mayflies were quick to fly into a mouth open for a yawn or a spoonful of rice. Whenever he spat, their dark bodies came out, too.

It was all because of the crumbling garden wall. That was the reason he had to share his home with all of this. So he made up his mind to rebuild the wall. He would build it strong and intact, a wall nothing could penetrate. If he could, he would burn down the thicket, too. Fill in the pond with soil, smooth it out, plant lettuce seeds. Then throw away all the lettuce.

He clenched a fistful of brick dust from the failing wall and said, "Look at this shit. Even in this bad a shape, we still can't rebuild it without clearing it with the government first. Just a stupid wall . . . All because of that fucking tomb. Who cares who's buried there anyway?"

His gaze fell on the prostrate burial mound. In addition to the ones in the tumuli park, there were another thirty or so scattered throughout the village. The entire village had been designated a historic district. As residents, they had to obtain government permission for any structural repairs, to say nothing of rebuilding. After all, more cultural properties could be buried underneath.

Even if he were to unearth the world's oldest equestrian figurine from under their house or an earthenware jar predating the relics on display in museums, he was better off not telling anyone. He had memorized the text of the Cultural Protection Heritage Act that was posted at the entrance to their neighborhood. It stated that all excavated artifacts were the property of the state, but the cost of excavation was the responsibility of the property owner. If you were stupid enough to report a find, the full cost of digging up the artifact would fall on you while the item itself would be snatched away by the government. If you were suspected of damaging or smuggling out an artifact, you could find yourself in a prison on the outskirts of D City without the benefit of a trial.

There was a time when every shovelful of dirt had turned up relics. That was before D City was designated a city. So much ground had been dug up that D City had resembled a plowed field before planting. Their own neighborhood had been built on land that was pockmarked with dig sites before it was all tamped back down again. It was said to have become too expensive to dig anywhere, as relics would turn up every single time, so instead they'd simply patted down all of the earth nice and flat. Whose corpse or what burial goods were interred under his house, he had no idea. There was no way of knowing whether what lay beneath him was a king's riches or a centuries-old mummy or the bones of those massacred during the war.

Near their house, a highway connected the port of D City with

U City and P City. An endless procession of container trucks made their way along it. Every time a truck passed the house, the ground would shake and emit a sound like the earth cracking open. If daylight in the village belonged to the mute, recumbent tombs, then moonlight was the time of the quaking highway. The villagers were used to the noise. It was just another feature of the place, no different from the rounded bellies of graves. If not for the noise, it would have been filled with an eerie silence, as if the village itself were a grave. Night was well-suited to noise.

He decided to begin work the following night. A truck carrying bricks was scheduled to stop by close to midnight. Bricks he had purchased at half price would be snuck into his house in cardboard boxes to make it look as though a relative living in another city had sent him gifts. A manager at the brick factory sold bricks on the sly this way. If he were to report his plans to the authorities, then he would have to purchase bricks with a stamp showing they met industrial standards and with proof that all taxes had been paid, and he would have to entrust the work to laborers contracted through the Cultural Heritage Administration and pay them by the hour. Of course, getting approval for the work in the first place was a pain in the ass. Not reporting any of it to the authorities was much simpler and cheaper. He wasn't about to go through all that hassle just to build one damn wall.

His neighborhood was already more than forty years old. The houses, which had all been built at the same time, were gradually losing their functionality as homes. Water leaked through sagging roofs, rooms wouldn't get warm even after fires were relit. Sewer water backed up through the cracked concrete in the garden every time it rained. But no one could make repairs to their home without getting permission first; the government even offered rewards for reports of unauthorized repairs. The reward money wasn't much—enough to cover the cost of your kids' snacks but not to actually justify ratting out your neighbors. There was no point in putting your house on the market, because it would never sell. Realtors who occasionally tried to do business in town would soon close, blaming the recession. But the economy had nothing to do with it. The only way out of D City was to make money somehow and abandon your house when you left. The people who lived there prayed that their neighbors would never leave, never fix their houses for the purpose of leaving, never make money. They rushed to inform the authorities whenever they found out about illegal construction, and on the rare occasion someone actually got an offer, they would sabotage the deal by demanding that the buyer pay the difference between the sale price and full market value.

He lowered his voice and said, "We'll have to work at night to keep the neighbors from finding out."

His wife nodded. In D City, that was a given.

*

In the darkness of the thicket, insects were screeching, excited by the night air. The hogweed, its roots firmly planted in the red mud, peeked over the wall. The plants had to be well over seven feet tall. An invasive species that had made itself at home there, its stalks were as thick and strong as bamboo. The roar of passing trucks hung in the air; the trucks could have been equally close or far. The house shook ever so slightly. His wife's gaze followed the lights of the trucks as she asked loudly, "This L person, can you trust him?"

L was the one who had told him about the manager at the brick factory and his under-the-table dealings. Annoyed at the volume of his wife's voice, he stomped purposefully out to the garden. The rodents that had been scurrying beneath the veranda held their breath as if alarmed by the sudden stomping. He went to the center of the garden and noisily worked the manual water pump. The rusty pump gave off a sour, metallic smell. He shoved down on the handle as hard as he could; water poured into the metal basin. The water was freezing. D City had been so hot that afternoon that simply standing outside felt like a struggle, but once the sun went down everything had turned frigid instead.

"He's a U City person now," he said. "I can't trust anyone in *this* town."

His wife lowered her voice, as if reminded by the noisy pump.

"That's the problem. L moved to U City from here. Can you really trust him? I heard he was able to leave this place and move there because he got reward money. Everyone's saying he sold someone out."

He leaned as close to his wife as possible and said, "We have no choice. Who else but him could get us what we need?"

All he owned was a shovel with a dull blade and an old pickaxe with a loose handle. Everything else he needed for construction he had to buy or borrow—from the bricks, cement, sand, and gravel to a drill that didn't make too much noise. His wife shrugged and walked slowly back to the kitchen. Her shadow filled the kitchen window. After her parents died, she'd put on nearly a hundred pounds. The sudden weight gain had ruined her joints and her digestion. Her arms and legs hurt all the time, and she suffered from arthritis and muscle aches. She had to eat constantly to satisfy her distended stomach. She reminded him of a soft, pulpy mollusk, a snail with its trail of slime. And in fact she moved as slowly as a snail and left a trail of crumbs and food smears everywhere she went. He watched his ever-expanding wife for a moment, then went inside.

Their child, who'd been staring at the TV, studied the blue bruises in her flesh in lieu of a greeting. The bruises made the child look even filthier than she was. When she was born, he hadn't been sure at first who the child took after, but now it was obvious. His child took after his wife. He never went anywhere with the child. Their one and only outing together was when he'd gathered up the newborn and brought her from the hospital to this house where his wife's parents' corpses lay.

He worked for the government office that managed the twenty-three tombs in the tumuli park. It was a special contract position with the Cultural Heritage Administration. Children who came to the park ruined the grass with all their running around. They would hide behind things and jump out, startling him. They left trash in hard-to-find places and peed wherever they pleased. He hated children.

Back when the tumuli park was built in the 1970s, there'd been plans to put a wall around it. Construction had just begun when another grave, thousands of years old, was uncovered. It was older by hundreds of years than the stone-mound tombs with their wooden burial chambers. They said fifteen more were found where they had planned to build the rest of the wall.

He muttered to himself as he ate his dinner, which had grown cold. He had no idea what was so special about wooden-whatever stone tombs or how ancient they were supposed to be. Everything he knew had come from the information posted next to the ticket office at the park. As for the ages of the grave goods on display that had been excavated from the twenty-three tombs, he'd had to memorize those.

"What if there's a bunch of ancient stuff buried under our wall, too? Maybe we should hold a memorial service before we knock it down and dig everything up? What if the king was assassinated and is still mad about it? How do you appease an angry ghost?"

He barely got the last word out before his wife threw her spoon at him. The spoon, smeared with rice, hit his left eye. The child giggled. His wife was convinced the spirits of her dead parents had become hungry ghosts and were clinging to their child. "Shameless ghosts, got nowhere to go so you bother an innocent child. . . ." And yet, despite those words, she never touched or patted the girl. He picked up her spoon from where it had fallen in front of the door. His wife was already eating again, using his spoon. He knew better than to mess with her. At the slightest provocation, she would beat the child until her anger cooled. If she was angrier than that, she would beat him too. She was terrifying in her violence. But even scarier than her was their child. When the child couldn't take another blow, she would bite his wife's arm.

He lowered his head and shoveled cold rice into his mouth. He pictured a large golden crown strung with half-moons of blue-green jade. He'd first decided to repair the wall because of the rodents. But now he was beginning to grow excited at the possibility of taking down the garden wall and unearthing a king's treasure. His house had been built on the flattened grave of an ancient king. There was no telling what lay buried there. The corners of his mouth lifted into a smile. He silently stuffed the rest of the rice into his mouth and thought only of the construction that would begin tomorrow. His stomach was full, but he didn't feel sated.

*

The truck that was supposed to arrive around midnight didn't show. But he didn't need the bricks yet anyway. Nor did he need any of the other things just yet—the gravel, sand, cement, drills, et cetera. To build a wall he would first have to take down the cracked and collapsing one.

When his wife asked how he expected to take the wall down without power tools, he said he'd thought about it and realized it wasn't a good idea to use any. Even if L offered to loan him some, he would have to say no.

"So what're you going to do? Knock it down with your fists?" She muttered under her breath that it was a mistake to trust L.

"I can't use power tools. The neighbors will hear them and come running. I just have to take it down a little at a time, day by day, with as little noise as possible."

In his effort to avoid his neighbors as well as the authorities, the work had become complicated and demanding. Demolishing a wall as quietly as possible. Buying bricks under the table. Manually mixing just the right proportions of cement, sand, and gravel to make concrete without the aid of a truck mixer. And doing it all at night when no one was around and the noise from the highway was at its loudest.

"It's easy. Just think of it as putting one brick next to the other in a straight line."

L had told him that building a wall was as simple as stacking matches. To move to U City, L had repaired his own house and sold it. When the sale had gone through successfully, the villagers had quietly lamented—why had no one noticed the illegal construction, why had no one blocked the sale, why had he been allowed to earn a living unhindered?

"Walls are easy. Put a line of rectangular bricks on flat ground. Spread a bunch of cement on it. Before the cement dries, put another line of bricks on it and add more cement. Keep doing that, and before you know it you've got a wall. But don't forget that in D City even the easy work is prohibited. That includes repairing a broken wall or replacing the manual pump in your garden with a water pipe."

L had pitched his voice low to underscore the risks.

He decided to use the shovel he already had at home before the rest of the equipment arrived. He waited for the night to grow dark before bringing the metal edge down on the bricks. The wall was solid. It didn't budge no matter how hard he hit it with the shovel. He put the shovel down and kicked the wall. His foot ached. He kicked and kicked, but in the dark he couldn't tell if what he was kicking was the wall or his wife or the rodents or the hogweed poking its many heads into his garden. He kicked at everything. The headlights of passing trucks revealed clouds of dust coming off of the wall. He used the pump to spray water on the brick to settle the dust. The wall crumbled more readily after it was wet. He soaked the bricks first, then used the tip of the shovel to chip away at them. If only it had rained, the whole process would have gone much more quickly, but the sky showed no sign of precipitation. It was hard work having to manually pump water to spray on the wall. That morning, the pump had spewed groundwater with great force, but by evening there was barely a trickle. On top of which, the water that splattered him was unbearably cold.

The work continued the next night. He wanted to get the wall up as quickly as possible. He wanted a strong house that would keep out weeds and bugs and rodents. He wanted to burn the colonies of weeds, all of them, that made it impossible to tell where his house ended and where the marsh began. He wanted to dig up the tomb behind his house and use the dirt to fill the marsh. Better still would be to abandon the house altogether and run. He wanted to follow L to U City. Or P City or K City. It didn't really matter where.

He resumed chipping away at the wall silently. He was thinking of telling his wife to pull the weeds from the tomb behind the house the next day, to get some exercise that way.

"It's just a grave," he muttered to himself as he worked quickly with the shovel. "It keeps D City fed. It keeps us fed. . . ."

He tried ramming the cracked wall with his shoulder. His body ached unbearably. He could feel a dark bruise growing beneath his shirt. A truck rattled noisily on the highway. With each truck that passed, the garden filled with light and darkened again. The ground-shaking noise continued. The night was a repetition of light and sound growing near, then far.

*

Then it was the next day and the next again, but still the bricks didn't arrive. His wife was so eager for the delivery truck to show that she could barely sleep. During the day, she would avoid leaving the house. He tried not to get anxious about it. And he still hadn't knocked down the entire wall. What he needed most urgently wasn't bricks but water. He asked his wife to please spray water on the wall while he was at work. It wasn't much help. The water evaporated too quickly in the afternoon sun. When he arrived home, he saw she had attached a long hose to the kitchen tap and was seated with the hose pointed at the wall and her gaze fixed outside the front gate. More water fell on the weeds than on the wall. Waterlogged weeds were craning their necks to peer inside the garden. Water from the hose had also leaked onto the garden and pooled there. The hose hadn't been tightened properly. Even his wife's bottom was drenched. Despite the leaks, the hose did fulfill its purpose. The work was progressing much more rapidly now that he didn't have to keep stopping to pump water. He would spray with the hose in his left hand and strike the wall with his right. The wall was leaning noticeably now, but the overgrown thicket still held it firmly in place. The weeds were guarding the house much more securely than any wall. No one could get inside the house that way.

Whenever he needed a break, he would climb to the top of the burial mound. It was just high enough for him to see over the wall and into his house. He could see where the plain-tiled roof had been patched with slate as well as the front gate, locked tight. The house lay on its belly in the dark. Between the dense tangle of weeds and the collapsing wall, it resembled a grave, long-abandoned and dilapidated. When he thought of it that way, he himself was no more than a cemetery watchman or a stonemason chipping away at the stone figures standing guard at a long-forgotten grave.

He'd never once climbed any of the tombs in the tumuli park. That was forbidden. Children his daughter's age were constantly clambering up and down them. His job was to blow his whistle and shake his club at them to try to make them stop. He couldn't run up after them or they would say "You're climbing up here, how come we're not allowed?" All he could do was stand at the bottom and blow his whistle and shake his club. The children would take their sweet time climbing to the very top and sliding down. At the bottom they would scatter. He would be chasing after multiple kids at once only to catch none.

He wore his creased hat and his dark yellow uniform with the armband that declared him the watchman. He spent a lot of time blowing fiercely on his whistle. Yet no one feared him. The kids seemed to know he wasn't a "real" employee. He feared these children who felt no fear of graves. But mostly he feared the graves. Because there was no telling what was hidden inside. At the same time he was grateful. Thanks to them, his family was able to live.

Most of the villagers made good money from the tombs. There were families who survived the whole year off a single day's work selling grass to resod tombs on Cold Food Day. The public works project of weeding the tombs was a source of livelihood for the elderly who had no children to support them. Many others set up tiny stalls in front of the tombs scattered throughout D City and sold cotton candy and iced tea. Others sold souvenir replicas of unearthed grave goods. Truth be told, the tombs were their sole livelihood.

*

It took more than a week to finally bring the wall down. Now all he had to do was dig up the concrete foundation, pour a stronger one, and—as L had instructed—stack bricks one by one. His wife gathered the crumbled old bricks and dust into a sack and dumped it all in the marsh. The marsh took its sweet time sucking down the dust. On one of her trips, she very nearly fell in. She grabbed on to the hogweed there and pulled herself to safety, then burst into tears. She'd been screaming her head off, but he hadn't heard a thing. The echoes of his shovel hitting the bricks were louder than her screams. The rumbling of trucks along the highway was louder.

The thought that he was finally digging up the foundation had him excited. When he lifted away pieces of the foundation, soil as soft as flesh would emerge. Soil soft and wet from groundwater that would slip gently through his fingers. What secrets were hiding there? What did the soil harbor? Picturing it made him happy to tackle the next task.

In order to excavate solid concrete, he had no choice but to use the pickaxe. To muffle the sound, his wife lay down an old blanket she'd soaked in water. The work progressed slowly. It wasn't easy to break concrete with a pickaxe with a loose handle. Hanging off the veranda, the work lamp he'd plugged into an outlet in their bedroom was too bright and hurt his eyes. He closed them and relied on his other senses to aim the pickaxe. Water from the blanket splashed his face.

The bricks still hadn't arrived. He would be needing them soon. The factory manager had asked him to be patient; demand for the unlicensed bricks had outstripped demand for licensed ones lately.

The more the wall had come down, the closer to the house the weeds had grown. The number of rodents and insects getting in had increased dramatically. The power cord for the lamp had fly tape attached to it at ten-inch intervals. Each strip of tape was thick with insects. Every morning his wife changed the tape.

The rodents now came and went as they pleased instead of having to sneak through holes. His wife set traps everywhere. The traps did catch a lot of them, but they would run around the house anyway, with a trap hanging from an ankle or their necks. They would stride about under the veranda, dragging traps behind them. One trapped rodent tried escaping to the marsh. They managed to catch a few of the slower ones. His wife would pick them up by the tail and fling them outside the wall. The stench from the marsh grew worse with each passing day.

*

At last, he'd nearly finished excavating the concrete. Whoever had poured the cement for the foundation must have made the formwork too shallow. With such a weak footing, the wall was bound to fail. He called loudly to his wife, saying that he was finally done. She wasn't there. It seemed she hadn't yet returned from throwing trash in the marsh.

The tip of the pickaxe struck a round pebble. He let out a happy shout, as if he'd already found grave goods. Breaking up the thin layer of gravel was much easier than working on concrete. He swung the pickaxe slowly. The drone of insects sounded like music. The stink wafting from the thicket didn't bother him at all.

He let out a long exhale, tightened his grip on the handle of the pickaxe, and brought it down hard. Something cold struck his face. He thought at first it was blood. He was sure he'd hit himself in the foot, but his foot didn't hurt. Also, what touched his face wasn't warm the way blood should be. Under the lamplight, it looked like the dirty yellow of urine. It was sewer water. He'd struck the sewer line.

The sewer water wouldn't stop spewing from the hole he'd made. He was quickly drenched. He shook himself and tried covering the hole with the blanket. The water immediately soaked the blanket. It kept coming, seeping all over the garden and flowing toward the weedy thicket. The tall hogweed was gulping it down excitedly. He tossed the pickaxe aside. No king's treasure or traitor's skull was to be found here. The only thing buried beneath his house was a sewer line carrying filth and waste. He had to get away. He decided to go to the top of the warm burial mound and rest there a moment in the headlights of passing freight trucks. One stupid sewer leak didn't mean his entire house was going to fall down. The whole way up the grave his body shook, and he slipped several times.

Despite the fountain of sewage, his house, enshrouded in darkness, seemed as peaceful as any other day. The weeds were still guarding the house as well as any wall. He remembered again that his wife hadn't yet returned from throwing trash into the pond. She had scolded him before for not hearing her call for help when she'd slipped into the water. He got up and descended the mound in the direction of the pond.

He pushed his way through the stiff stalks of hogweed. Small, fine thorns pricked at his palms. He heard a tearing sound and assumed his clothes had snagged on the tips of some branches. By the time he made it to the water's edge, he was exhausted. He saw nothing there. No sign that anyone had been there either. As he turned to leave, his eye caught a whitish, roundish object floating in the water. It looked different from the usual clumps of rotting leaves or the blackened, floating bodies of dead rodents. Maybe it was the body of that woman who'd drowned all those years ago. Or maybe it was just a giant mound of trash.

He felt around for a long stick and held it out toward the object. It was too short to reach. He moved closer. Just as he thought the tip of the stick had touched the object, he realized one of his feet was slipping and carrying him down into the pond. He groped for a foothold, figuring the water would come up only to his knee. His toes touched nothing. He lost his balance and fell.

The water was up to his waist. To keep things from getting worse, he braced his legs as firmly as he could. To his surprise, he lost his balance and began to tip over. He flung out his arms toward the large object lying stubbornly with its back to him. He needed to grab something to remain standing; he would use it to pull himself to safety. His fingers sank into it. It was as billowy as white bread. He grabbed on tight. At the force of his grip, it rolled over. His wife. She was staring wide-eyed at him, as if to say what a shame they should meet like this. Equally surprised to be meeting her here, shocked to see her dead with her eyes open, puzzled as to when exactly she'd died, and startled she was still staring at him, he let out a shriek.

His shriek didn't make it past the wall of hogweed that ringed the pond. If a truck arrived, he would have to scream as loudly as he could that he'd fallen in. With that thought, he clung to his wife.

He stared at his house with its demolished wall. He couldn't tell where the house ended and the marsh began. Was sewer water still spilling into the garden? Between all that sewage flowing beneath it and the pond being so close, the foundation never stood a chance. He could erect the strongest foundation in the world, but because of that constant seepage of underground water, the day would come when a crack would appear, the wall would start to shift, and he would have to take up the shovel and tear it down. He would never be able to build an impenetrable wall.

Little by little he was being sucked deeper into the marsh. He'd always meant to measure just how deep it was, but he never imagined he'd do so with his own body. He tried holding more tightly to his wife only to slip, lose his balance, and sink in farther. He raised his head and looked up at the weeds that seemed to have grown as high as the roof. The thicket would grow denser by the day, and the marsh would continue to rot. The frogs feasting on his and his wife's tattered flesh would sing louder, more raucously. The rodents that ate those frogs would attack people fearlessly. Up to his neck now in the muddy water, he inched closer to home.

—Translated by Sora Kim-Russell

PARADE

The trouble started with the elephants. Originally from Laos, they had just recently been transferred from the Songdo amusement park, which had a magnificent Ferris wheel that towered two hundred feet in the air and never stopped spinning from the time the park opened in the morning to when it closed at night. If you timed your ride right, you could watch the Yellow Sea turn bloodred at sunset.

Twice a day, the elephants would put on a show in the middle of the park. First, all six would raise their trunks in unison to greet the visitors, then the youngest would dribble a soccer ball. Another would unfurl the Korean flag with its trunk to great applause. The show ended with a dance party, the elephants swaying their enormous bodies in time to music. Weekends were packed with families and couples, but weekdays saw nearly zero guests. They had once performed to a crowd of fewer than ten people. Before each show, the elephants had to parade around the park to draw in spectators.

That day the sun set earlier than usual. The red waves of the sea where the sun had begun its descent cast their glow onto the parading elephants. The two bringing up the rear came to a sudden halt. The four in front kept going, the sunset at their backs, but the other two flapped their ears like giant fans and directed their heavy steps away from their usual route. When the elephant handler, likewise from Laos, noticed and approached, the elephants took off running, and the handler had a hard time catching them. Since it was a weekday, with few guests, there were no casualties. But the park management put an immediate halt to the elephant parade and show. All six elephants were sold to U Park on the cheap.

U Park put the elephants to work the very same day they were transferred from Songdo. The plan, if all went well, was to make them the park's new mascots. Another large theme park had opened nearby, and the search for a mascot had gained in urgency because of it. The competition had an artificial savanna where lions, tigers, bears, zebras, and other large animals were allowed to roam free. Visitors rode in cars through well-maintained wilderness and watched the animals go about their business. Lions and tigers mingled freely and would pause to turn and stare until the passing cars were out of view. Bears loped along on all fours, then stood on their hind legs to walk or to clap their front paws together in thanks for the army biscuits the drivers would toss to them. The sheer size of the competing park made it truly world class. It also had the country's longest, steepest roller coaster. The same glorious red as the sun, it was given pride of place in the center of the park. The coaster featured a vertical drop, two full loop-the-loops, and another vertical drop right at the end like an exclamation point.

This competing theme park was blamed for U Park's decline. U

PARADE

Park hastily replaced the lights in all the restrooms with brighter lights. The cafeteria, which had been criticized for its lack of cleanliness, received brand-new tables, chairs, and tiles. But nothing really changed. The restrooms remained as dark and fly-ridden as ever. The cafeteria tables were still crusted with food. If not for the local kindergartens' group reservations, weekdays would have been all but deserted. With no one to ride them, more and more rides sat idle. The pirate ship ride shook and screeched loudly. Passionless screams wafted from the roller coaster. Compared to the country's longest coaster, U Park's was no better than a child's toy.

The six elephants wore colorful cones on their heads and glittering capes. Though popular with park guests, the lions and Mt. Baekdu tigers couldn't exactly participate in the parade. The same went for the clever monkeys with all their little tricks and the flocks of flamingos with their painted-looking bodies. Elephants were better suited than any other animal to marching in a parade. They moved slowly and were large enough to impress spectators.

Walking beside the elephants was their Laotian handler, dressed in the same gold-trimmed white uniform as the brass band that led the parade. They were followed by floats as big as tanks. And bringing up the rear was a long line of hired marchers dressed as fairy-tale characters.

K, E, P, and S marched toward the front of the parade. None of them had ever been this close to an elephant before, and they kept their distance. When the handler saw this, he tried to wave them closer, gesturing for them to pat the elephants. All four shook their heads in unison and said in English, "No, thank you."

"The dumps those things take are bigger than the dirt piles at a construction site. They never wipe their asses either. Have you ever seen an elephant wipe its ass? The shit slides down their legs, and they even sit in their own shit. All that stuff stuck to their legs, that's dried shit."

K plugged his nose with his fingers. The handler shrugged and said nothing. What actually bothered K, though, wasn't the smell or their dirty legs. It was their size and the toughness of their hides. If he happened to stumble mid-parade, he'd be trampled. He moved a little farther away. The other three followed suit to create more space between themselves and the animals.

As usual, they were dressed like the Town Musicians of Bremen. K was the donkey, E the cat, P the dog, and S the rooster. They called each other Donkey, Cat, Dog, and Rooster, and in his donkey mask K really did look like a donkey. Now and then he'd let out a loud, braying laugh that made his cheekbones jut. E, who was allergic to cat fur, had suffered worsening allergic attacks since donning the cat mask. Whenever P was drunk, he'd bark like a dog. Even without the mask, S's face was as bright red as a cock's comb.

The Town Musicians of Bremen weren't popular storybook characters. Most of the kids had no idea who they were. Every time K walked past, they would yell "Donkey!" in English, mistaking him for the character from the animated movie. Rooster was mocked because the cock's comb he wore on his head drooped like a wet rag, nearly covering his face.

The four of them had spent the season dressed as animals, but soon the Town Musicians of Bremen would be put away. New characters would be chosen, and they would have to dress accordingly. They had no idea who they were going to be. Their boss said only that they had to be characters who would appeal to today's preschoolers.

*

Every day the parade began with an earsplitting burst of music from a tape deck installed in one of the floats. Donkey would raise his flute, Cat his drum, Dog his violin, and Rooster his trumpet. Mere toys, none of the instruments sounded like they should. But from inside his mask K would fill his cheeks with air and mime playing the flute anyway. The flute never made a sound whether his cheeks filled with air or not. S would pretend to play his trumpet, his fingers moving over the valves. Clacking away at the valves was all he had to do. The tight, plastic strings of P's violin would squeal. E had to be a little more careful. If he hit the drum hard enough, it would let out a dull thud that carried, so he only pretended to hit it. In fact, he could have pounded away. The recorded music was so loud that none of the spectators would have ever heard his drum anyway.

In the dressing room that day, the four had put on their masks angrily. Their boss had been yelling at them again. He'd unloaded on K especially hard: K didn't smile enough and was late all the time.

When K had come running in, panting for air, their boss had said, "With a mug like yours, where do you get off coming in late every day?"

K was breathing too hard to hear him.

"I'm so sorry. There was an accident on my way to work."

The boss glared at him for a long moment, then lowered his voice and said, "Wipe that anus off your face."

"Huh? What did you just say?"

"Anus. Rectum. Asshole. Your face is so wrinkled and pouty it looks like an anus."

K's face flushed deep red. The others, who'd been lined up in front of the mirror to practice smiling, all froze. They held their breath, faces still locked in smiles, and watched K to see what he would do. They prayed he'd control his temper and do nothing. At the same time, they hoped he wouldn't just take it but would have a go at the boss. They meant both things.

K frowned as if to demonstrate. His face filled with wrinkles.

"Is this the anus you're talking about?"

Laughter erupted among the marchers, and E let out a loud guffaw. The boss thought they were making fun of him and lashed out at E instead of K. But that didn't stop E from smirking any-way. K was scolded for not looking happy enough, and E for look-ing too happy. The rest of the parade workers got scolded, too, either for smiling too much or not smiling enough. As soon as the boss left, one of the younger men glared at K and clucked his tongue at him.

"Some role model you are."

Incensed, S took a swing at him. While others rushed to pry them apart, voices were raised and soon everyone was shouting and screaming at each other.

Before ending up in the parade, the Town Musicians had worked at all kinds of jobs, from construction and moving com-panies to selling water purifiers, telemarketing insurance, and even multilevel marketing. Part-timing in a café too, though that hardly qualified as backbreaking work. Of course, it wasn't just one person who did all this. K had done manual labor on construction sites, and P had moved furniture. E had gone from telemarketing to the lowest level of multilevel marketing and was promoted twice, which he'd achieved by roping his whole family and all his friends into the same scheme. S was the one who'd worked part-time in a café. Though he'd had to do all sorts of menial chores, including fetching the owner's cigarettes, it was nothing compared to the other three. All four of them would go on about the part-time jobs they'd held, bragging about who'd had it worse. If one mentioned a hardship he'd suffered to earn money, another would scoff and say, "Is that all?" They spent their breaks comparing who had lived a harder life and which of them had endured it better.

The parade was held twice daily; the rest of their time was spent doing odd jobs around the park. They had to put up with measly paychecks. They had to put up with their boss's high-handedness and niggling rules. Worst of all, they had to put up with their own smiling faces in the mirror.

Smiling was their boss's main concern. He paid no mind to the parade's lack of a theme, the poorly made masks, the lousy keeping of time, or the disorderly rows of the marchers straggling behind the floats. He was convinced the success of the parade depended solely on the marchers' smiling faces and exaggerated gestures. Sometimes he ordered them to spend the entire day practicing their smiles. They'd gone along with this grudgingly at first. But the rule about smiling applied whether they were wearing masks or not. The boss told them that if they weren't smiling, then the masks weren't smiling. As if to mock his claim, the masks never stopped smiling. The marchers would don their masks, raise their arms, and wave them back and forth. When they encountered children, they would lean over and say, "Hello! Hello!" repeating the word twice to every child. When they encountered very young children, they would offer a balloon if they were carrying one, or a hug.

All that smiling meant, when they stopped, their normal facial expressions looked so angry they couldn't help but laugh at themselves. Being in a bad mood felt like a mockery of their smiling selves. People meeting them for the first time liked the marchers. But it was never long before they found themselves being told to wipe the smile from their face and stop pretending to be nice.

That day, the Town Musicians of Bremen did nothing right. Donkey K wore a constant frown inside his mask. He was so angry that instead of playing along with the flute music blaring from the float, he held his flute up to his eye and peered through it like a telescope. E banged on his drum completely out of time to the music. Even though he was dying of anger, he realized he was still smiling, his eyes curved in half-moons and the corners of his mouth hiked up. Feeling himself smile like this, he banged harder on his drum. P held his violin at his waist like a guitar and plucked the strings instead of using the bow. S marched in silence, his trumpet hanging limply at his side. None of the Town Musicians spun in circles with their arms outspread or high-stepped merrily with their knees raised. Nor did they bother to wave back at the children who waved at them. They scurried ahead to avoid being trampled by the elephants behind them. In silence, the six elephants followed the Town Musicians like enormous wooden puppets.

*

They were almost to the third song when the ground began to shift. P had slung his violin over his shoulder. S kept pushing his mask up. It was an unusually hot day. He had to get a little air on his neck or he'd collapse from the heat. He thought he felt the ground tremble. E, who'd been banging on his drum haphazardly, wondered if it was an earthquake. It felt like somewhere deep inside the earth was slipping ever so slightly. Then he thought maybe it was just a little vertigo. S's hand shook, making him drop his trumpet. As he bent to pick it up, he realized a massive yet subtle movement was passing through him. The shaking continued when he straightened up.

What they took to be an earthquake turned out to be the elephants. Frightened spectators fled from the stampede. Children ran hand-in-hand with their parents. Some, knocked off their feet by the crowd, were dragged on their knees. Babies screamed. The shocked crowd wondered if what they were seeing were runaway elephants or really trams in the shape of elephants or life-size elephant puppets.

No one was able to stop the six stampeding elephants. According to later reports, they ran without stopping at speeds of up to twenty-five miles per hour. The animals' handler ran after them as fast as he could. As if by some prearranged plan, the elephants raced out the front gates and crossed all eight lanes of the highway outside the park. No elephants were hit by cars while crossing, and no people were trampled by the elephants.

Once outside the park, the six elephants headed for a nearby mountain. They raced straight there as if that had been their destination all along. Despite the occasional rumor of wild boars, it was closer to a hill than a mountain, not a great hiding place for something as large as an elephant. As long as they were there, catching them would be only a matter of time.

Opinions were split on the elephants' sudden escape. There was nothing particularly special about that day. The sea at sunset hadn't turned the marching elephants bloodred as had happened in Songdo. As usual, spectators threw snacks for the elephants, some hitting the marchers instead. Also unchanged were the flocks of pigeons that flew down to scoop up the fallen snacks. The clanging brass band, the gold-trimmed uniforms, the plodding marchers, the sweat dripping behind their masks and the sour sweat smell wafting from them, the disinterested faces of the park guests, the balloons lost by children watching the parade, climbing higher on the wind—all were the same as every other day.

The handler readied tranquilizer darts. No telling what agitated elephants might do. Squads of police were brought in for the public's safety. The police surrounded the mountain. It was low and easy enough for someone walking at a leisurely pace to reach the top in an hour. Search teams spread out to look for elephant tracks. Everywhere the six elephants had passed, the grass was flattened in the shapes of their enormous feet. The search teams followed the footprints but soon realized it was futile. The prints crisscrossed over each other and then suddenly stopped, as if the elephants had risen straight off the ground. Then, a long way off, the prints turned up again.

The elephants themselves didn't turn up, though. Someone asked if the elephants had maybe escaped to some other place instead, but no one listened. Of course the elephants had come to this mountain. There were witnesses. To a person, they all excitedly reported having seen elephants running toward the mountain. And the firemen had video of the elephants hiking up its slopes together. The colorful capes made them impossible to miss despite the poor quality of the video. Even without the capes, though, they would have been unmistakable. It wasn't every day you saw six elephants parading around in the city in broad daylight. After several days the search team had turned up nothing, so more police were sent in. Still no elephants were found. Their whereabouts remained a mystery.

*

With the guests gone for the day, the park filled with a queer silence. The elephant cage lay empty. The Town Musicians had finished straightening up the practice room and were on their way out when they decided to stop by the elephant cage. No one was there; the handler must have gone home already. The four of them climbed onto the gate. A foul smell filled the air.

Animal psychologists had offered different hypotheses regarding the elephants' disappearance. One had suggested that maybe a pigeon scavenging for crumbs on the parade grounds had pecked an elephant's foot and the elephant, spooked by the sharp beak, had taken off running, and since elephants are such social creatures, once that one started running, the rest had followed. The news reported that the elephants were abused during training. The proof was that they had been put to work in the parade immediately after being relocated from Songdo. More reports followed regarding the tendency for animals kept in metal cages to compulsively harm themselves. A chimpanzee had been observed eating its own vomit and throwing it up again. Some elephants were known to obsessively sway their bodies back and forth and side to side. Ostriches would pull out their own feathers, and giraffes would chew on the metal of their cage. Sympathy toward animals kept in captivity swelled. Opinions on animal welfare were offered, but ultimately no serious inspection was carried out. Everyone was confident that once the elephants were located, this would all blow over.

But the escaped elephants couldn't be found anywhere. The search party had broken into teams to scour the mountain yet again. At one point, someone called quietly, "Found one!" Searchers poured in from all directions to join him. Faintly visible through the trees was a large, gray animal. The searchers steadied their breaths and aimed their tranquilizer guns. The animal took twelve darts before finally falling with a *thunk*. A searcher waited until the animal's movements slowed before creeping up and throwing a fine-mesh net over it. Squirming under the net was a wild boar. They'd spent so many days covering the same ground they'd forgotten what animal they were searching for. Or maybe the boar had resembled an elephant. All of them were afraid of seeing an actual elephant. If one appeared in front of them, they weren't even sure they'd be able to tell whether it was an elephant or a boar. Their fear grew so intense, they worried they might mistake each other for an elephant and be shot with a tranquilizer dart.

Thanks to the elephants, the park was now crowded with new visitors. U Park had promised to take responsibility for any damage they caused and to find the elephants as quickly as possible to ensure no humans would be harmed. As a gesture of remorse, they vowed to cease all animal parades, not just elephant parades, and to do everything they could to make sure nothing like this ever happened again.

All of the marchers had gone their separate ways. K took a temporary gig in the park's haunted house. He liked it; he said it was a perfect fit for someone as bad at smiling as he. Dracula K's job was to hide in a coffin and frighten people by opening the lid and popping out at them. Sometimes when he popped out of the coffin, he let out a braying donkey laugh. Little kids were terrified of K in his vampire costume because, unlike the other vampires, K smiled too brightly and made strange sounds.

E and P were put on janitorial duty. While sweeping, they would wave to the little kids who tossed their candy wrappers wherever and greet them twice: "Hello! Hello!" During their breaks, they would made the children laugh by putting their brooms between their legs and pretending to be witches.

S was put to work on the roller coaster. He was nice to every-one, and when he saw children, he leaned over and waved with both hands, each time imagining he was still part of the parade but wearing the mask of a ticket taker. For S, life was always mid-parade.

Out of the blue, P asked, "Those elephants, where the hell did they go?"

"Beats me," S said darkly. "They say there are wild boars on that mountain. Do you think the boars ate the elephants? Seeing as how they still haven't been found."

"Do boars eat elephants?" E asked, making a face. He had to grimace to keep a smile from sneaking into place.

P, too, frowned to keep from smiling, "If they did, wouldn't they have found the bones? Not even a boar could eat elephant bones."

As if in response, the metal gate they'd climbed onto swung open. It hadn't been padlocked. The four of them climbed down and stepped into the elephant cage. The floor was crusted with feces.

"If I had to live here, I'd run away, too," P said.

K hesitated a moment then ran off, saying he'd be right back. The remaining three stared silently after him and then sat in the elephant cage. Though they were sitting on elephant dung, it felt more like a warm cushion than something dirty.

After a long moment, K came running back, out of breath. He was carrying the flute, drum, trumpet, and violin. He wiped the flute against his pants. Then he held the mouthpiece to his lips and began to play. With each puff a raspy sound came out. The plastic flute seemed to shine in the moonlight. E banged on the drum. The dull thud echoed through the air. S puckered his lips. A quacking, splitting sound came out of the trumpet. P plucked the strings of the violin with his fingers.

The four of them left the cage and went over to the dumpster behind the management office. There they threw their instruments into its dark, open mouth. They listened as the violin fell onto the rest of the trash and were turning to leave when they heard the long, gruff cry of an animal somewhere. K and S mimicked its call. E and P did, too. Suddenly, E took off running. The others followed. A custodian with a flashlight chased after them, blowing his whistle. They ran for a while and then stopped in unison and blew through their hands at the custodian. *Bambara-bababam!* Then, like the six elephants, they ran without stopping through the employees-only gate. The custodian's whistle grew fainter and fainter.

Once outside U Park, they weren't sure where to go. Across the highway was the mountain where the elephants had gone. The mountain crouched low in the dark like an animal. The four of them stopped to catch their breath. Then they slowly headed for the subway station. Ready to whisk them away to the center of the world, the enormous subway train was just arriving.

*

The elephants were eventually discovered inside a bunker right in the middle of the city, hidden behind an old green metal door. The door was near a flower bed across the street from the main office of a stock brokerage. No effort had been made to conceal it with plants or a screen. The door had always been there, though no one knew for how long exactly. That was why no one had ever regarded it with suspicion. One office worker in particular had walked by the door every single day without realizing it was there. At most, a handful of people had stared at it and wondered where it led, but even they had simply concluded it must lead to a storehouse or an underground passageway built there by mistake. It was a completely unremarkable door, a door like any other, with paint peeling off and rust spreading.

The first to question the door were some employees from the Department of Construction and Safety who had been studying a cadastral map of the area to prepare for the construction of a bus transfer station. One of the employees knocked on it. The door emitted a faint ringing sound. Particles of rust clung to his hand, but knocking gave no clue as to the world beyond it. There was no telling what sort of door it was, what it would reveal when opened. The door was keeping its mouth as firmly shut as the fist-sized padlock that was dangling from it.

The employees began by thoroughly examining the maintenance logs for the substructure in order to determine whether the site had ever contained an underground passageway. It had not. They came back with a pair of bolt cutters to break the rusted lock. But they couldn't bring themselves to go through with it. They feared the unknown lurking inside. Instead, they pried the door open a crack and inserted an endoscope.

The first things to appear through the endoscope were large, dark shapes. The shapes sometimes moved together as one and sometimes broke apart. Because they couldn't tell what these enormous shifting shapes were, they feared them. The employee who had first asked about the door let out a sigh, wondering how he'd gotten himself into this.

As the image on the screen sharpened, the outline of one of the large moving shapes grew clearer. It was an elephant. Judging by what could be seen on the screen, there were at least four of them in there. No one could believe they were really elephants; they couldn't peel their eyes from the screen. But it was true, they were elephants.

The supervisor remembered then that a while back six elephants had escaped from U Park. Though that didn't make it any easier to understand how the elephants could have wound up in there. They contacted U Park. The person who answered assumed it was a prank and yelled at them. The supervisor, who could hardly believe it himself, sent the person a screenshot. At last the old door was opened. The park officials, the Laotian handler, and six container trucks to carry the elephants waited outside. Just inside the door was a long set of stairs leading down to what looked like a bottomless pit. The darkness hid the base of the stairwell from view. They thought they could hear an elephant trumpeting somewhere. The handler descended the stairs cautiously. When he reached the bottom, he found himself in a cavernous space of almost four thousand square feet. It even had a toilet and kitchen. Holding court in the center, as if it were the owner of the place, was a heavy leather sofa, white with dust. And there were the six elephants standing around like furniture. The elephants looked up at the light seeping through the open door. But they soon looked away and slowly ambled around the bunker as though out for an afternoon walk.

It seemed strange the elephants could stroll around like that underground without any noise or vibration leaking out. But that wasn't the only strange thing. There was no end to the questions: How did they get inside the bunker, how did they survive down there without starving, where had their colorful capes vanished to, and who on Earth had built the bunker in the first place, and when?

The park officials raised a stink, saying it was clear someone had hidden the elephants there for some nefarious purpose. They suspected the handler: who else would be capable of moving six animals of that size? The handler, being from Laos, either didn't understand the accusations or pretended not to. He kept petting the elephants, not so much happy to see them as glad to be returning to work. Meanwhile, the park officials were united in their opinion that the handler had planned the whole thing so he could sell the elephants for a tidy profit. Implicit was that the elephants couldn't possibly have hidden themselves in the bunker and locked the padlock behind them or been moved by anyone other than the handler.

As one by one the elephants boarded the container trucks, the enormous bunker was revealed to the public. Everyone was shocked, first at the sight of the elephants emerging from behind the metal door and then by the bunker the elephants were leaving behind.

No one knew when the bunker had been built. Some reports claimed it was built by a general who had held the presidency for decades through rigged elections and authoritarian politics. Others pointed out that it appeared to have been maintained until recently and the age of the building materials indicated it had to be post-dictatorship. No one could say definitively when the bunker was built, how long it had been maintained, or who owned it.

The bunker's metal door was locked again. People walking by would knock on it sometimes or fiddle with the padlock. They thought they could hear a long, low echo ringing behind the door. They thought they could hear the thud of heavy footsteps in there somewhere. As the dull thuds existing only in their imaginations faded away, all that was left was the door, as unyielding as silence itself.

*

The four had been about to leave the park when six trucks arrived. They stood and watched them pass.

"You suppose the elephants are all tied up in there?" S asked.

They had already heard what happened from their boss, who said the parade would be starting up again.

The truck at the front of the procession stopped with a wheeze. A flock of children in matching preschool uniforms crossed in front and headed for the exit. All at once, K clenched his fists and pretended to play a flute. The way his hands moved made it seem more like he was throwing punches at the truck. After the children had crossed, the six trucks continued on their way. K kept blowing his imaginary flute and throwing empty punches until the trucks were out of view.

The four went back to the elephant cage. It was still empty. They climbed the gate like before. The six elephants were scheduled to return to the stage after a few days of psychological evaluation. Then they would stand in a row and curl their trunks like donuts to greet the park visitors and kick soccer balls and rear up to walk around the stage on their hind legs. The louder the applause, the faster their heavy legs would carry them.

When the parade resumed, the four humans would be wearing new masks. Adept at smiling, E might find himself dressed like a prince instead of an animal—their boss had hinted as much. He regretted having lost his temper at E. As for himself, E was excited at the prospect he might not have to wear an animal mask, but at the same time he wondered if he wasn't better off wearing a mask, since the weather would be turning cold soon.

"But how'd the elephants get in that bunker in the first place?" K asked.

No one answered.

"Was it really the handler?" P asked.

"Not even he would have had the skill to get the elephants all the way there, no? And who would he have sold them to anyway in a country this small?"

At S's words, E nodded vigorously, and K pictured the elephants soaring through the air—winged elephants flying single-file into the underground bunker at the very heart of the city. K laughed out loud.

Just then a thunderous, earth-shaking noise rang out. S brought his hand to his chest. His heart had begun beating hard like an elephant's feet hitting the ground. He was panting. He steadied his breath and slowly climbed off the gate.

"Do you hear that?" K asked.

S realized with relief that the noise wasn't his racing heart. A shocked look on his face, P pointed to the mountain. Wavering there were the shadows of enormous animals making their way downhill. Elephants. As they drew closer, the four saw that the elephants had musical instruments dangling from their necks or curled in their trunks. One carried a flute, another a drum. Another had a trumpet, with its tricky fingering, hanging from its neck. They were marching slowly and, at a signal from the lead elephant, began to play their instruments in unison. None of the sounds were right. Delighted at the discord, the four laughed long and hard. Though they'd been smiling the whole time, somehow it felt like it was the first time.

—*Translated by Sora Kim-Russell*

FRIDAY HELLO

Kim dealt. Park took a quick look at his cards and placed them on the table. Cho hid his in one hand and fondled his chips with the other. As if on cue, all three met each other's gaze. The game had begun.

As they played, they poured beer for each other and shared snacks. They spoke a little, too. Cho did most of the talking. He was telling them all about the oil he used to fry chicken, from getting it to the right temperature to how he disposed of it when it was spent.

"I went to a chicken farm once," Kim blurted out at random, interrupting.

Kim described how the stink of ammonia was so strong he had to plug his nose and breathe through his mouth, and how dirty chicken feathers kept flying into his open mouth. Unfazed by the interruption, Cho switched to boasting about the problems with franchises. Kim interrupted him again to say that the chicken farm had reminded him of an apartment building. He said he understood why everyone compared apartment buildings to chicken coops and added that inside the chicken cages, which

111

were stacked on top of each other just like apartments, the chickens found their swelling bodies so unbearable that even after their beaks were cut off they would still try to peck at each other and at their own feet. As his story wore on, Park made a face. Cho swallowed his spit, as if to wash a bad taste from his mouth. Kim realized his faux pas and stopped talking. They resumed staring at their cards in silence.

Their games usually began around midnight on a Friday and ended somewhere around dawn. None of them knew why it had to be Friday; it just seemed like the right day for getting together. They were in their forties, the age at which you had to be glued to your job all week. Friday night was the only time you could unwind comfortably.

It was also a Friday when Kim had first randomly popped into the fried chicken place in front of the apartment complex on his way home from work. The stacks of *tongdak*, whole fried chickens, displayed in the window had tempted him in. He placed an order to go, a special treat for his daughter, and while waiting had a draft beer. The beer tasted watered down. Kim was sitting right in front of the TV set. A group of comedians were in the middle of a skit. Now and then the camera cut to the laughing audience. Kim wasn't a big fan of these kinds of rowdy comedy shows. He watched them so rarely it was impossible to understand the jokes.

The smell of frying chicken filled the air. It hit him then that his daughter didn't really like *tongdak*.

"What on earth are they laughing at?" Park had mumbled, sitting alone and drinking his beer.

The loud laughter of the audience sounded canned. Kim nodded in agreement.

"That's what I say too. What's so funny about it?"

The two men drank at their separate tables and idly watched the show. When one of the comedians came racing out onto the stage and tripped, they chuckled. The owner brought Kim his chicken. Kim took the chicken he'd ordered for his daughter and offered it to Park.

"Now *that's* what I call funny," Park said, gesturing at the TV. Kim nodded.

"Me, too. I don't understand everyone's idea of humor these days," said the chicken place owner. That was Cho.

Kim and Park were his only customers that night. The three of them drank watery beer together and watched the rest of the comedy show. Kim was a lightweight: he was already red-faced and chuckling at every joke despite not having drunk much. Every time he laughed, Park gave him a look. When the show ended, Kim invited the other two to come over to his place and have another drink. Park downed the rest of his beer without a word. He wasn't fond of fraternizing with strangers. Cho said he would head over around midnight after closing his shop. Park nodded slowly. That was his answer, but he wasn't planning on going. There was no harm in not showing up. Though they all lived in the same complex, he'd never spoken to these men before. He could run into them tomorrow and not even recognize them. And besides, Kim seemed drunk already.

Kim hurried home and told his daughter that Daddy's friends were coming over and to stay in her room even if it got noisy. She was in high school. There was nothing good to be gained from her poking her nose in grown-ups' business.

"You have friends coming over?"

"Just some guys from around here," he said.

"If they're just some guys, why are they coming to a stranger's home this late at night?"

"Beats me," Kim said. He honestly had no idea why either.

Park went home and sat on his sofa in the dark without changing clothes. The apartment had sat empty all day and was chilly. He kept the lights off so he could see the Han River Bridge below. The lights of the bridge sparkled prettily. The view alone was why he'd chosen this apartment. As he stared out the window, rapt, he thought to himself he must be the only person sitting alone at their darkened window on a Friday night looking out at that view. He changed into warmer clothes and headed to Kim's place.

Kim was dozing off on the sofa when Park arrived. About ten minutes later, Cho turned up. Though he'd changed clothes, his body still gave off the smell of oil and fried chicken.

Now that they were all together, they had nothing to talk about. They sat side by side on the sofa, gazed at the TV set that wasn't turned on, and drank beer. Kim looked at their reflection in the screen. Finally, one of them spoke. As if waiting for just that moment, one of them responded. Kim listened to the two men talk and laughed out loud like he was watching a comedy show. When he'd grown bored enough to think he'd rather be watching TV, someone suggested a game of poker. He wasn't sure exactly which of them had suggested it. Park was the one who said he liked card games.

"The thing about cards is, it comes down to how economically you handle all the variables with the different numbers and suits. Card games are intense and sophisticated. And creative."

It was the longest Park had spoken since they'd begun hanging out.

"Korean card games are more sophisticated than Western ones," Cho shot back.

Park replied that Cho just didn't understand the essence of Western cards, and Cho muttered that Korean cards had an essence, too. They went on that way for a while before they found themselves sitting together at a round table. Kim won the pot. He said that, since he won, drinks would be on him next time.

They met again the following Friday. Cho won and treated them to drinks. From then on, around midnight every Friday, they joined each other at the round table covered in a black cloth. Though they met every week, they never exchanged phone numbers. The only number they did have was for Cho's shop. They had no particular reason to call each other. Come Friday night, they naturally found themselves at Kim's apartment. After their game, they went to a sauna outside the apartment complex. In the high heat of a dry sauna room, they sweated out the night's fatigue. Afterward they ate tripe soup. Whoever had won the game was supposed to treat the others. This was usually Kim, but most of the bills ended up being paid by Park. Whenever it was time to settle up, Kim would disappear into the bathroom or fumble through his pockets for his wallet. Cho would hem and haw, so Park would step up without hesitating.

Cho was about to put down the card he'd just taken when the door swung open. Kim and Park looked up at the sound. Cho was a little slower. He needed time to palm the card. It was Kim's daughter. She stood in the doorway and glanced at each of the men in turn. Park and Cho had never seen Kim's daughter before.

She had never come out of her room to greet them. Kim had no idea what to say and kept staring at her in silence. If the police had raided them for illegal gambling, he would have found words to speak, but confronted by his daughter, he drew a blank. Just as he was wondering if he should make her say hello at least, she walked over and showed him a card. It was the ace of hearts.

"This was on the living room floor," she said.

Cho stared cluelessly at Kim's and Park's faces.

"What's that?"

It was Park who finally spoke. He gestured for the girl to bring him the card, and she handed it to him. He examined the card. She quietly left the room, closing the door behind her. Only after they heard the sound of her going into her own room did Kim's face start to turn red. Park set the card on the table. Cho got upset, as if he'd only just seen the card for the first time.

"What was that doing on the floor? Did one of you guys hide it there?"

Kim was taken aback. So were Cho and Park. It felt like their weekly game night had been instantly reduced to a sleazy gambling pit. Kim knew he had to say something if he didn't want to be misunderstood. This was his place. Regardless of who had planted the card there, he was the most likely suspect. The ace of hearts on the table glowed bright red like Kim's own racing heart.

They weren't much given to chitchat while playing. Cho would curse a little under his breath when the game wasn't going his way. Park and Kim were never bothered by his cursing, though, since none of it was directed at them. Mostly, they played lost in their own thoughts. They didn't say much as they considered their cards, nor did they study each other's faces to improve their chances of winning. They made no effort to keep their own faces serene or feign disappointment. The pot was always so small it would have been laughable for any of them to actually try to win. From the outside, it looked less like they were there to win money or build their friendship than simply to sit in silence and relax. Park and Cho chain-smoked from start to finish. Not because the game wasn't going their way or because they wanted to win but simply out of habit. They didn't spill their ashes carelessly on the floor. They were careful to tap them into the ashtray. Now and then Cho would hawk up phlegm from somewhere deep inside his chest. Their games were so quiet that was the loudest sound in the room. So it couldn't have been that their late-night gambling had awakened Kim's daughter.

Where the hell did that card come from? Kim was so distracted by his daughter bursting in and handing him a card she claimed to have found in the living room that he realized only belatedly she was still in her school uniform. A quick glance at the time told him it was after 3:00 a.m. He'd thought she'd been asleep in her room. It hadn't occurred to him that she might not be home yet. What on earth had she been doing out at this hour? What time did she come home? Come to think of it, he never heard her door open.

Kim made an effort to relax his face. He'd been so deep in thought he probably looked like he was trying to come up with a convincing lie. Feigning composure, he glanced back and forth between the cards in his hands and the cards on the table. Cho and Park looked at him and at each other. Their gazes weighed on him. He was worried they thought he was a card shark. Just his luck that he'd won most of the hands so far.

Kim had always been terrified of losing. Back in school he had gone to great lengths to avoid losing at recess. While the other kids were laughing and having fun, he was working himself into a sweat. Not that the penalties were so terrible. They mostly consisted of singing or dancing in front of the others, and if you refused to do either, then you could write your name in the air with your butt. Kim hated all of it. He didn't want to be shaking with fear as he sang. He couldn't bear to lose because he hated the idea of getting teased for being a bad singer.

He didn't know anything about the card his daughter had found. Someone was either playing a trick or had dropped it innocently on the way to or from the bathroom. Kim wondered if it was part of a ruse concocted by Cho or Park to put him on the spot. It could have been Cho, who took an awful lot of trips to the bathroom, or Park, pissed about losing every hand, playing a prank. But what did they have to gain from a stunt like that? Judging by the look in Cho's eyes as he stared at Kim and the way Park puffed coolly on his cigarette, it didn't seem either of them could be behind this.

As far as Cho was concerned, their games were just that: games. He never thought one of them might be up to something. Which wasn't to say Cho himself always followed the rules, of course. He would pretend to go to the bathroom in order to mess with the cards or to steal a peek at their cards when Park and Kim weren't looking. That was as far as he went, though. Just a bit of leverage to shake things up. Cho fought the urge to look under the table. He didn't want Park and Kim to think he was so easily affected by a petty ruse. Or maybe he didn't want them to think he was so stingy he would get upset over chump change.

Cho calmly studied Kim. He actually knew very little about the man. All he knew was that Kim's wife had died and Kim lived alone with his teenage daughter, that the apartment was probably owned by Kim as he'd lived there a long time, that Kim was a middle manager in his mid-forties at a medium-sized company who had a penchant for interrupting other people's conversations, that he was probably stingy judging by the fact that he'd bought a full order of chicken only on his first visit and phoned in half orders ever since, that he was a lightweight who laughed easily when drunk, and that he was bound to lose his job eventually and end up as a franchisee like Cho. Even while envying Cho for running his own business, Kim didn't exactly hide the fact that he was grateful to still be a salaryman. It was obvious Kim looked down on franchises—none of which were any better than the other—as the last stop for forty-somethings who'd been pushed out of the security of their salaried jobs by restructuring. Cho hated that attitude. He was convinced Kim would end up in the same place as him someday.

The idea that someone was up to something had Park thinking the game was getting more fun. So much so that he wished the deception had had a little more zing. He'd begun to grow bored at how serious and unchanging their game nights were. What amused him more than the deception, though, was the idea that someone would cheat just to win a little chump change. Of course, no one knew better than Park how chump change could be grown into a significant sum. He tried to feign indifference, but he couldn't hide the smirk on his face.

Cho tugged nervously at the black tablecloth and looked back and forth between Kim and the card. He glanced at Park now and then, too, as if seeking his approval. Park avoided Cho's eyes. A weighty silence descended over the table.

Park was the one to break it. "Shall we stop here and go to the sauna?" His voice was calm.

"Let's do that," Cho said. He set his cards down and followed Park away from the table. Kim stood reluctantly. They crossed the living room to the front door, concealing the awkwardness on their faces in the dark.

*

Kim slowly chewed the burnt toast. With nothing else suitable for dinner, he'd toasted some of the bread that he'd found in the freezer. But he'd misjudged the timing and it had come out burnt to a crisp. He chewed and swallowed the bitter bread. His mouth was bitter, but his heart was even more so. He'd lost an important account. One that his boss had kept saying the company's future depended on. Come Monday morning, the whole place would be talking about it. Kim was sweating already just thinking about it. It was mostly the fault of one of his subordinates. The person's prep work was sloppy and their ideas predictable; even how they dealt with competitors left a lot to be desired. At times like these, it was his job to reassure his subordinates, but he struggled to contain his anger. The truth was that he wanted to be thought of as a good boss. He preferred the ease of hanging out with employees to hanging out with his own boss. Since he too was stuck working under someone, he was hardly high up on the totem pole. But because he was a middle manager, the other employees didn't like him. They made no attempt to hide their displeasure when he suggested going out to eat together. One even lost patience and blurted out laughingly, "Look, boss, you can't just expect us to drop everything for a company dinner." The others agreed.

He said, "Who said anything about a company dinner? All I suggested was grabbing a bite together."

But the others countered that if the manager's there, that makes it a company dinner. And they all took off without so much as a sorry. If anything, they seemed to leave faster than usual, as if for fear he would stop them. Kim didn't know what to think. Though he knew there was no point in comparing, he couldn't help remembering his own early days at the company. He had never turned down his bosses when they called for a company dinner, even if it meant breaking other appointments or dates he'd made.

After the others had left, Kim sat alone in the empty office and flipped through the failed proposal on his desk. The cramped office, partitioned into cubicles, felt like a chicken coop. He thought he caught a whiff of chicken shit. He pinched his nose and shoved the whole proposal into the trash. How much longer would he have to stick it out here, feeling like his feet were being pecked at? He wanted a promotion, but the added responsibilities were a drag, too. To minimize failure, he made every decision based on what had been done before. The last thing he wanted was the responsibility and potential for miscommunications that came with any new decision. His subordinates saw him as old-fashioned and incompetent. Even his superiors saw him as stuck in his ways and tactless with his subordinates. They were all right about him.

There was just over an hour to go before midnight. He had no idea whether Park and Cho would show up. He hadn't seen them at all for the past week. That was a relief. If he had crossed paths with either, he might have hurried away in embarrassment. He had snuck a peek inside Cho's chicken place on his way home from work once. Cho was sitting alone at a table, watching television. There were no customers. After that, he took the long way around for fear of bumping into him. He never ran into Park, though. Park drove everywhere. Kim didn't know what kind of car he drove or his license plate number. If one of them had cheated, it couldn't have been Park. There was no way he'd have hidden cards just to win a little extra change. He seemed loaded already. But neither could it have been Cho. Kim couldn't decide whether it would be better to flush out the culprit or look the other way. If he brought it up again, they might think he was doing it just to cover for his own culpability.

If only his daughter hadn't surprised them with that card, maybe they would have enjoyed their game into the wee hours as usual. Kim set down the toast he'd been eating and opened his daughter's bedroom door. She wasn't home. Between her after-school classes and study sessions at a reading room, she wouldn't be home until well after midnight. He looked around her darkened room and pictured her tired face poring over a book. He immediately felt ashamed of himself for doubting her and assuming she had an ulterior motive when she'd come in with the card. As if a mere child could have an ulterior motive. His wife had died in a car accident when their daughter was on the verge of becoming a teenager. Afterward, she had become very quiet and prone to shyness even around her father. The older she got, the more Kim was at the age when he had to work harder and harder to keep from being pushed out of his job. The more years he added to his resume, the shakier his position at the company. Likewise, with each new school year, the busier his daughter became with after-school and supplemental classes. Kim had grown increasingly estranged from her. Sometimes he even forgot what grade she was in. He'd quickly given up trying to remember what she wanted to be when she grew up, what kinds of things she liked, what her best friend's name was. Those weren't things you could learn instantaneously or figure out from just a few questions. Sometimes while watching TV she would laugh or frown, but he never knew what made her laugh or caused her to frown or who she hated and who she liked.

Her bedding still retained the impression of her body. He considered straightening the sheets and making her bed for her but decided against it. The cleaning lady came on Mondays and Thursdays. Kim didn't want his daughter to know he'd been in her room. He examined her desk. The shelf was crammed with workbooks and reference books. He pulled one out and flipped through it. The workbook might as well have been brand-new, it was so untouched. He wasn't too surprised by this; he'd been the same way back in his school days. After returning the workbook to its place, he went through her desk drawers. The first drawer held a jumble of pens and notebooks. He'd heard that kids these days were into collecting random things. Maybe her thing was collecting pens and notebooks. He opened all three drawers in turn.

He searched the rest of her room, too, but learned nothing about his child. He'd found unused worksheets and a drawer full of untouched pens. Aside from that, he saw nothing else and learned nothing. Her calendar made no mention of her friends' birthdays let alone her own, his birthday, or her mother's death anniversary. Like a skilled thief, the girl had wiped her room clean, leaving behind not a single trace of herself. She didn't even have one of those little diaries girls her age usually kept. It suddenly hit him that the only thing he really knew about his daughter was her name. And while he'd been losing touch with her, all he'd been busy doing was gradually getting pushed out of his job.

*

Cho stared intently at the screen. Ten horses were running and kicking up dust. They raced forward, their knees bending and straightening like clockwork. Cho's feet moved, too, as if he were running with them. His feet clip-clopped beneath his chair. Cho's horse had pulled ahead at first but was steadily falling behind. His heart racing, he inched closer to the screen. He wished he was doing the whipping instead of the jockey. Thirsty, he gulped down the beer he'd bought at the convenience store. But it didn't slake his thirst. Whenever he was thirsty like this, he felt an urge to drink the bloody water he'd soaked the raw chickens in. Not that he had any intention of drinking blood. It was just something that crossed his mind whenever he felt he couldn't go on living without doing something outrageous.

It was the same that morning. He'd received a call from the bank. He should never have tried to grow the business. He'd borrowed too much. The monthly interest payments were exorbitant, and the rent had doubled from what it used to be. He'd had the idea to put in more tables, change out the seating, and lower the lights to bring in more drinkers, but it didn't result in more customers. People were losing interest in fried chicken. Not long ago, some sort of bird flu had gone around. Day after day, there were images on the news of dead chickens and ducks being buried in mass graves.

Frequenting the off-track betting site didn't help. When he'd first started betting on the horses, luck had been on his side. Luck was reserved for the few. Every time, he thought he was one of them. The person sitting next to him punched the screen and cursed in frustration. Cho glanced at the familiar-looking man who never took his bloodshot eyes off of the screen. Clearly, this was a person who'd been gradually slipping out of luck's good graces. Cho's horse fell to the back of the pack. He didn't leave until he'd spent all the money in his wallet.

His wife tallied the week's sales just as she did every Friday.

"We made almost nothing this week," she said with a frown. "We'll have to catch up this weekend."

She closed the ledger and added water to the keg of draft beer. He didn't tell her about the call from the bank. When Cho had lost his job as a middle manager to corporate restructuring, his wife had hurriedly looked into fried chicken franchises. She'd talked Cho into it despite his reservations. Fried chicken didn't require secret recipes. All you had to do was season the meat, batter it, heat the oil to the right temperature, and fry it for the right amount of time. The head company took care of the interior of the store. Cho was in charge of frying the chicken. He fried chicken from opening to closing in front of a display window that faced onto the street. He stacked the chickens, fried to a golden brown, in the window like bait. Whether drawn to the sight of those chickens or the smell, people would always glance inside as they walked past. Each time, Cho felt like he'd been turned into a chicken. Like he was standing naked out in the street, plucked of every single hair. He should have been accustomed to the work by then, but he still burned his hands on the hot oil all the time. When blisters formed, he would pop them by pinching them between his fingernails. Then he'd drop another battered chicken into the hot oil with no time to feel the pain. It saddened him how he had to stand in a window frying chicken while burning his hands on the oil just to make a living. The smell of the oil gave him headaches. If business didn't pick up, he might have to throw himself into the hot oil like a chicken just to eke out a living. He might have to nail metal shoes to the soles of his feet like a horse and race full-tilt with blinders on, kicking up dirt.

Cho soaked the raw chicken in water. The blood leached out, fresh and reeking of iron. He placed the chicken he'd soaked the night before in a sieve to drain. When that was done, he seasoned it and set it aside; after the seasoning had soaked into the meat, he dipped the chicken in batter.

A man who looked like Kim went by outside the window. Cho opened the door and started to call to him but stopped. It could have been a lookalike. Though they might have crossed paths before, once they began hanging out on Friday nights they never bumped into each other by accident. They'd met for the first time in Cho's shop, but after that Kim and Park never came in to buy chicken. For all he knew, he might not even recognize them in broad daylight outside the apartment complex. How had he ended up hanging out with them at all?

Park didn't seem the type to socialize with guys like them. Cho had been to his place once, back before their poker games had started. Park had ordered chicken. Friday nights were busy. The part-timer hadn't returned yet from making other deliveries, so Cho had no choice but to take the box of fried chicken to Park's place himself. Park was standing there quietly in his darkened apartment, dressed in a suit, waiting to receive the delivery. The Han River Bridge was visible from the large picture window in the living room. The lights of the bridge were beautiful. He gazed out at the scenery while waiting for Park to pay. They lived in the same complex, but all Cho could see from his own apartment was floor after floor of lighted windows on the other buildings. The sight of it made him feel the walls were closing in.

He wondered if Park remembered. Even during their games, Park would just sit there silently and stare at his cards. Now and then he would respond to whatever Cho and Kim were saying with a smile of agreement or a frown of disapproval, but he never contributed to the conversation.

Cho slid the battered chicken into the heated oil. A drop of oil splashed onto his right index finger. The inside of the store grew hotter. The chickens were cooking to a golden brown. Cho's face was cooking, too, to a deep red. His wife had written the number of chickens they needed to sell that weekend on a large piece of paper and taped it by the window. Cho stared at the number. The debt and interest he owed the bank, the money he'd lost at the track, the fried chickens he needed to sell—the numbers kept getting all tangled up. While adding more chicken to the oil, Cho scuffed his foot against the floor as if he were grinding down a horseshoe. He wished he could spur himself straight out of the store. It was Friday.

*

Each time he exited the bank, he felt the week draw to a close. The feeling was followed by a surge of relief at the thought of another week safely behind him together with light regret that the time had gone by so quickly. Fridays were when he put money into his wife's account. The money was always gone by afternoon. The regular withdrawals were proof his wife and son were okay. But Fridays were also the day he wondered most about how they were really doing.

She kept asking for more and more. She said the older their son got, the more there was that their son had to do and wanted to do. Park could measure his child's growth through the escalating sums of money he sent. While their son was suffering growing pains in a foreign country, he was suffering financial pressure. He considered calling his wife but thought better of it. The intervals between calls from his wife had been increasing more and more. It had also been a long time since he'd spoken to his son, who had started playing after-school soccer. Park knew full well it was easy for people in his position to give in to despair. To avoid that, he made a point of wearing the finest suits with crisply ironed shirts and eating only in clean restaurants at proper mealtimes. Having to choose different foods to eat every single day was supremely annoying. The more embarrassed he felt about eating dinner alone surrounded by others eating with companions, the more slowly he would chew his food.

He spotted Cho on a side street leading to the apartment complex. Cho was passing his car on a scooter, though it might not have been Cho. It might have been the part-timer who did most of the deliveries. The scooter quickly disappeared among the buildings. Park gazed at the back of the scooter and muttered to himself that it was Friday again already. The only thing the three men had in common was that they lived in the same complex. Park had never lived in anything other than an apartment. It was his opinion that apartments were the ideal living space. Despite the common assumption that apartments were identical, the truth was that each was completely different on the inside. At the same time, everything was the same, which meant that no matter where you went, you never felt out of place. That was how Park defined individuality in modern times. Being too different was off-putting, but being too alike was shallow. Even before their Friday get-togethers, he had noticed Kim and Cho while out for a stroll on the walking paths in their complex. Park's memory was sharp. All three of them had been meandering around alone. While Kim looked depressed, Cho had looked excited about something. Park knew Cho owned the chicken place in front of their complex. Cho was always standing in the window, frying chicken and staring blankly out at the street. Cho was also the one who'd delivered chicken to his door one night. He hadn't left right away but stood staring out at the view.

When he'd stopped by Cho's shop for a beer, Kim was there, too, watching TV by himself. The moment Park saw him, he recognized him from the walking paths. He'd also seen him in the sauna in front of the complex. Kim's body had looked as red as raw meat.

Cho would have liked to talk money with Park. Nearly no one knew the true state of Park's finances. The amounts coming in and going out were so big that even Park got confused. He'd made a lot of money from aggressive investments, but he'd lost even more. The economy had been changing to more and more extreme forms of speculation. Now the only way to survive was by fattening yourself up. Just as you needed animal senses to survive in gambling, it took animal senses to predict the flow of capital. Rational, objective judgment gave you ground to stand on and kept you motivated, but it didn't actually help you choose. Choices always came down to intuition. Park believed the economy grew by virtue of chance, not reason. He used his imagination to make investments, and he earned and lost money. His work consisted of placing a bet and then waiting to see what would happen, leaving the outcome to chance. Chance took no notice of personal ability or effort. Nor did it take into account wealth, whether inherited or acquired. In that respect, nothing was more democratic than chance. Park was well aware that the word "democratic" was inevitably accompanied by the word "unfair."

The truth was that he enjoyed his Friday nights with Cho and Kim. Their interests were different from his, as was the amount of money they made and how they spent it. There were no issues he had to discuss with them and no worries he had to share. And so, every Friday, Park went to Kim's apartment. When he was with them, friendship wasn't business, it was life. This was a pleasant and yet unfamiliar feeling for him.

*

Kim arranged a pack of cards and poker chips neatly on the table and set an ashtray in the middle as if to mark the exact center. Then he took the seat nearest the door. This was his usual spot. Park always sat to his right and Cho to his left. They might not come. It wasn't exactly written in stone that they had to see each other on Fridays. The only specifics they had agreed on were midnight and Kim's place.

The week had passed quickly. As usual, Kim had come home late from work. His daughter was likewise busy with after-school classes or supplemental classes or some other plans he knew nothing about. Kim hadn't forgotten about the little misunderstanding from the previous Friday. Though it had only been a week, it felt like it had happened ages ago. He carefully checked the living room and bathroom. There were no fallen cards on the floor. He looked up at the wall clock, feeling the tiredness on his face. Midnight was approaching.

Park confirmed over the phone that the money had been withdrawn. The recorded voice informing him of the small amount remaining in his account sounded like a friendly greeting from his wife and son. He tried adding up the number of Fridays he'd sent them money but drew a blank.

"Everything okay?" Park mumbled, gazing down at the lights of the Han River Bridge.

He thought he heard a voice respond, "Of course everything's okay." He stood there a moment longer, then changed clothes and left to go to Kim's place. He left all the lights on to dispel the chill of the empty apartment.

Cho pressed hard on the doorbell, as if by doing so he could erase the figures floating around in his head. He'd be spending the next day frying chickens and staring at the number posted on the wall, so he wanted a little peace and quiet for at least what was left of today.

Kim opened the door and welcomed him in. His smile was as bright as always. Cho waved at Kim, then at Park. Park looked cheerful. Cho rattled off apologies for being late and sat to the left of Kim.

"So, how was your week?" Cho asked, looking back and forth between Kim and Park.

Park said he'd been busy as usual but otherwise good and lit a cigarette. Kim said he'd been a little under the weather. Cho nodded and said that at their age being busy was a good thing. Kim asked Cho how his business was going.

"Seems like chicken is all anyone eats anymore, because I've spent the entire week frying nothing but chicken," Cho said with a laugh.

They all smiled at each other. It felt like it had been exactly a week since they'd last smiled like that. At last the week had ended. His face glowing, Kim dealt the cards.

—Translated by Sora Kim-Russell

LOST AND FOUND

Park kept a tight grip on the handle of his shoulder bag. The train was more crowded today and he would have rushed if he'd known, but now it occurred to him that, even if the streets were congested, he'd have done better to take a taxi. It was because of the bag. There was a memory card in it and documents protected in an envelope so the edges wouldn't get crumpled. He was supposed to deliver them to Song on his way to work. What would Song's expression be when he received them? Park began to wonder as he was pushed into the train by the crowd. What would be the best way to deliver them? The most important thing was that Kang not find out. Kang and Song were not on good terms, and any unnecessary misunderstanding was to be avoided. Park clutched his bag more firmly. The strap was worn out and so frayed he worried what would happen if it broke and the bag was lost. He regretted not having bought a new bag. The one he had looked too shabby for carrying important documents. Someone shoved his way past him toward the door. Park clutched his bag more tightly, careful not to get swept into the crowd. He was barely able to find a seat by the time they passed the transfer station. Park pushed aside the person in front of him and sat down. He held the bag on his lap over his tightly closed legs.

He wasn't tired enough to sit. He hadn't been able to sleep last night, but he felt more refreshed than other days because he had finally finished what Song had asked him to do. Now all that was left was to go through the formalities. The man standing in front of him gave him a disapproving look. Park opened his newspaper to avoid his gaze. The newspaper featured a major story about last night's earthquake. It said the earthquake was the eighth largest in recorded history. The shock was intense enough to crack the walls of apartment buildings and knock things off shelves. The quake was so strong it was even felt in the city where Park lived, though that was far from the epicenter. Last night he had been preoccupied with the work he was doing for Song and hadn't been aware the ground was shaking. Even if he'd known, he would have thought it was because of the vertigo he'd been experiencing all the time lately. Park had finished working on the documents and put them in the envelope only to remove them again. He'd reviewed them dozens of times already, but he still wasn't sure he hadn't missed some errors. He checked all the figures over and over. Song had a short fuse. When he found an error, he would scream, "Aren't you even capable of spotting a simple mistake?" Song's twisted face was still vivid in Park's mind.

"Haven't you been pushing yourself too hard?" Park's wife asked, handing him his bag.

Park glared at her with his bloodshot eyes. She smelled like she'd been nursing. She was a wet nurse for someone else's infant, taking care of the baby while the mother was at work. People must have thought she was reliable because there were endless requests from the women in the apartment complex. His wife had never raised her own baby, but she had been a wet nurse for such a long time she gave off the aura of being a mother. Sometimes the baby was still there when Park got home from work. It would burst into tears when it saw him, perhaps because he was unfamiliar. The infant made the apartment feel stuffy.

"Could you maybe stop taking care of babies?" Park asked.

"I told you it helps keep me from being bored, and I'm making good money," she said as she saw him off. "I told you, if you really can't stand it, I'll only do it until you get your promotion."

Park got into the elevator without responding. He didn't know whether she wanted to work because they didn't have enough money to live on or simply because she was bored. In the mirror on the elevator wall was a man with bloodshot eyes and a haggard face. Park examined him. The man in the mirror gripped his bag more tightly, as if he were self-conscious.

It had been a week since Song had called him in. Park had gotten the message from Kim.

"Song wants to see you," Kim whispered into his ear as if he were telling a secret.

Park hastily grabbed a notebook to take notes. Kim gave him a light tap on the shoulder. "What could it be?" What made Park uneasy was Kim's pat and not Song's sudden summons. Park hurried to Song's office with long strides.

"Come have a seat."

Song gestured with his eyes toward the black leather sofa. Then he walked over to the door and pressed the locking mechanism. The click was incredibly loud. Park quietly put his hands together. He was sure he had done something wrong. He remembered the documents he had submitted to Song. Park wasn't very meticulous. There must have been some errors in the accounts.

Song took his time and sat across from Park. There was a rumor that, when he was angry, Song had a habit of throwing whatever was within reach at his subordinates. Park quickly scanned for objects that could be thrown. There were several: a crystal ashtray, a pencil holder, black accounting files, a telephone. It was also said that Song had once been so angry about figures not adding up in a report he had stabbed a pen through the back of an accountant's hand—Choi, from the department next door. Actually, Choi tended to exaggerate quite a bit. But still, Park felt himself lightly stroking the back of his hand. Song, hands clasped together with his fingers interlaced, leaned forward and gestured for Park to come closer. Park moved to the edge of the sofa.

"As you know, there's going to be some reorganization coming up," Song said.

Park held his breath and nodded. Song had terrible mouth odor.

"I'm going to recommend you as the team leader this time."

Song looked at Park. Park straightened his hands like a bored student and pressed his legs together.

"I know it hasn't been especially quick for you," Song said.

Park lowered his head slightly. Most of his coworkers were already team leaders.

"But it really shouldn't take you so long, you know."

Now Song nodded his head as if he were sympathizing. As a clerk, you can't be the best at everything, but that doesn't mean you have to be the worst. If he failed this time, even the junior employees would push him around. Song withdrew a thick file folder from his desk drawer.

"So what I'm saying is, get this done quickly for me."

Park held his breath and scanned the documents.

"This job is going to be a bit tricky," Song said.

Even from a quick glance at the material, Park could see what it was Song wanted him to do. It related to the company's cash flow and wasn't entirely legal. "As you know, I don't give this kind of responsibility to just anyone."

When he heard that, Park suddenly felt sad. The truth was, up to that point he had always been "just anyone."

"You'll be helping the department and—more broadly—it's about growing the company. So don't worry. Do you think you can do it?" Song said.

Park lowered his head, pretending to look at the documents, but really he was contemplating how he should best reply. There was only one possible answer. From the outset, there was no way he could possibly say no and, therefore, the important thing wasn't the answer but how long it took him to respond. The longer it took, the less likely Song would be satisfied.

"Of course," Park said.

The words, which had been stuck inside him, seemed to leak out of his cracked throat. Song was staring at him.

"'Of course'? Does that mean you'll do it?" Song said.

Park nodded his head vigorously. It disturbed him that his voice had cracked. It also bothered him that he'd unintentionally let Song's question steep for too long before answering.

"I thought someone in your position would be happy to help out."

Song casually stood up from his seat. Park gathered the files together and got up. Song gave him a tap on the shoulder as he left the office.

"I'll try my best," Park responded, as if confirming Song's gesture.

"This is a very important matter," Song said. "Do you get my meaning?"

Park nodded as he stood by the doorway. He was confused. Was Song saying he should consider himself lucky to be entrusted with such an important task? Was it a sign that Song found him particularly trustworthy? Or was he just warning him not to tell anyone?

Song lowered his voice. "You tend to keep your mouth shut, don't you?"

Park nodded again. The important thing was to keep his mouth shut. As he left Song's office, Kim gave him a look, but Park turned away, pretending not to notice. Kim obviously knew something. The sudden pats on the shoulder and sidelong glances said as much. Had he done this sort of thing many times? Was that the reason he'd been promoted so often? In that case, could he tell Kim about it? Park was lost in thought as he pretended to organize the chaos on his desk. Recalling Song's tone of voice when he asked him about keeping his mouth shut, Park abandoned the idea of confiding in Kim.

Park had been afraid Song would never call on him, and that anxiety made him remember now how it felt to be alone with him. It seemed more unpleasant than pleasant—and repulsive rather than just unpleasant—and as Park tried to determine which feeling was more tolerable, he realized Song was a deceitful con man.

Then he worried that Song might have detected his realization. Park wanted to tell him he would be glad to play along and could go even further, but with a sidelong glance into Song's office, he swallowed the words. It was nothing to joke about, so it would be better not to joke about it. Park tended not to tell jokes because he was afraid they'd be taken seriously.

He'd chosen to remain silent rather than see his words lead to unnecessary misunderstandings. As a result, he always seemed overly serious and obstinate, and it was hard for him to get along with people. This was even more true with his supervisors. They were uncomfortable around him. Park knew himself to be sincere, but he wasn't exceptional. He was often scolded by Kang. His proposals were frequently rejected. Song repeatedly ignored suggestions he made during meetings.

Park vowed to wash away any notion of his incompetence by finishing the job neatly. His promotion was tantamount to the company's approval, an acknowledgment, for the time being, of Park's value. His wife would stop caring for the baby, as she had promised. That would also put an end to the stifling atmosphere at home created by the humidifier and the heat. Park used to volunteer to work overtime because he didn't want to go home while the infant was there. If he got the promotion, he wouldn't have to work overtime any longer, so he could go out for walks with his wife in the evening when the breeze was cool. With a pleased expression, Park put the bundle of materials Song had given him into his bag.

For several days he stayed up all night doing the favor Song had asked of him. The work wasn't easy to complete. There were more nights when he lost sleep. One night, when he'd fallen into a deep slumber, he was awakened suddenly by the sound of the baby crying. It was after the baby had already been returned to its home. Park looked at his wife, who was asleep, unconscious. She was babbling, her fists clenched as if *she* were the infant. Park got up and went back to work on the documents. He grew so tired he became increasingly quiet at work.

"Don't you think you've become a bit too taciturn?" Kim asked.

"Yes. I think something must be going on lately," Han said from the next desk.

"I'm just a little tired." Park yawned.

"Doing a job for Song is usually like that," Kim said. He was trying to comfort Park.

Han nodded. "I've heard that a lot, too. You can handle it."

Their lame attempts at being supportive annoyed him.

"What would you guys know about it?" he said. "It's usually not that hard."

Kim and Han returned to their seats looking embarrassed.

The announcement for his station stop came over the speakers. Park roused himself and hurried to make it through the door before it closed. The nap, short but sweet, left him even more tired, and his steps were heavy. He could still see Kim's embarrassed expression floating over the heads of the people going to the turnstiles.

"I'm so exhausted I can't go on," Park muttered in a voice still thick with sleep.

"Doing a job for Song is usually like that," Kim's voice seemed to be saying from somewhere. Park clenched his fists as if in agreement. He heard the sound of something rustling and being crushed.

It was a newspaper. There was no bag.

*

The station office clerk checked with the train Park had been on and contacted him to say no bags had been left behind. Park had no way of knowing whether he had left his bag or someone had taken it while he was asleep. After reporting it to the station's Lost and Found, he went straight to the nearest police station, stumbling several times along the way. Suddenly, the ground was trembling and seemed to rise up in front of him. He couldn't tell whether it was the ground shaking or if the shaking was in his head—or even whether these were aftershocks from the previous night's earthquake. Park massaged his temples nervously.

"Just report it to the Lost and Found," said the policeman in the rumpled uniform.

"Someone lifted my bag while I was asleep. Isn't it your job to investigate theft?"

Park grimaced from the constant pain in his head. The policeman finally opened his black notebook and asked him for a description of the bag. When Park related that the bag had a worn-out strap and lots of scratches and scuff marks, the policeman gave him a look that said, *Who would even steal a bag like that?*

"What's in the bag?" he asked.

"Papers. Documents," Park answered loudly. "What was lost was the documents. It wasn't the kind of bag where the strap would have fallen off."

"Is there something else?"

"You just have to find the documents," Park said. "That's what's urgent."

"You need to tell me everything that's in the bag," the

policeman said, annoyed. "Otherwise, how can we confirm it's yours and give it back if it happens to turn up?"

Park tried hard to visualize what was in the bag. Maybe his wedding ring was in it—he wasn't sure. Unable to resist his wife's nagging, he left for work every morning wearing it. One day, in the elevator, he'd taken it off and put it in his bag. Other days he would put it in his pocket. He'd gotten so used to taking his ring off that he couldn't remember exactly what he'd done with it that morning. He rummaged through his pants pockets and found an old credit card slip. Maybe he hadn't even worn the ring because he was so focused on the paperwork. It might still be on the vanity. His new glasses and the leather wallet he'd had for three years would probably be in the bag. He wasn't sure. He always kept those things nearby, but lately, more often than not, he'd had trouble finding them. They could be on his desk or in a drawer in his office. Those other items didn't seem significant because he'd lost the documents. Song had instructed him not to leave a trace of them anywhere. He'd followed those instructions and transferred all the documents from the computer onto a memory card.

Which was also in the bag. Park grew angry at himself for following Song's instructions so timidly.

It was after rush hour and the lobby elevator was empty. A man approached and stood next to Park. Park looked at his cell phone nervously. The Lost and Found or the police station might be contacting him. His idea of handing the papers off to Song on the way to work burst like a bubble.

He would have to go to Song and make excuses for not being able to do the job he'd been instructed to do. He might even have to ask for another copy of the documents. It was morning, so Song would be in the executives' meeting. The topic of the meeting would determine Song's mood for the day. If Song was in a good mood, he might be able to tell him the work was delayed and that, if he gave him another copy of the documents, he would get the job done even if he had to pull an all-nighter. For all he knew, the bag might turn up before he even broached the topic. There were plenty of people in the world who wouldn't touch other people's belongings. And, in any case, the documents were all just numbers and obscure codes. Whether someone had picked up the bag by mistake or stolen it, they would have no use for such papers. And, for that reason, they might have ended up being tossed in the garbage. From the garbage heap, the papers would find their way into the hands of a junk dealer and be recycled. Dense with numbers and codes, they would become wrappers to keep hot rolls from getting cold. And to think, those were the documents that were supposed to help the department and grow the company. Park burst out laughing.

The man in the elevator with him glanced at Park. For some reason, Park couldn't stop smiling, and he finally broke into laughter again.

The man followed Park into the office. Kim, Han, and Shim greeted him loudly. The man who'd followed Park in raised his hand in reply and entered Song's office. Park turned to Kim, who was looking at his computer monitor.

"Who's that exactly?" he asked.

"Are you nuts?" Kim replied brusquely before turning his attention back to the monitor.

Park's desk looked directly into Song's office. Through the window, Park saw a man enter the office and take a seat. The man soon stood up and spread open a newspaper on the table. A moment later, he walked over to the phone. The phone at Han's desk rang. Han hurriedly answered it.

"Yes, sir. Yes, yes, I understand."

Han hung up the phone and rushed into Song's office. A moment later, a young man appeared at the window. Park lowered his head below the partition. When he looked up, the blinds were drawn in Song's office. Park panicked when he realized the man had been Song. It was because he'd been pushing himself too hard the last few days. The whole time he'd been looking through the documents, he'd had a headache and a mild case of nausea. Maybe it was because he hadn't been wearing his glasses. He was tired and couldn't see clearly, so perhaps that was why he hadn't recognized Song at first.

Park spent the whole morning calling the Lost and Found centers at each subway station. When asked to describe the bag, he would hesitate. Even though he'd always carried it, he couldn't remember its shape or size. He was even confused about where the strap was wearing out. When asked to describe the lost item, he said to one place that it was just a briefcase, and to another that it was a wallet with cash, a notebook, a ring, and some papers. Park also called the police station. He was told that the police were too busy to look for a lost bag.

Anxious that he would never find the missing bag, Park chided himself for pretending he didn't know Song and forgot he had paperwork due to the marketing department later that day. The marketing person called him at the end of the day and reprimanded his negligence in a highly critical tone. Park also forgot about his appointment to meet with a client. It was Kang who answered the call from the client long after the appointed time.

"Didn't you know how important today's appointment was?" Kang scolded Park.

Park hung his head. He started to make an excuse about losing his bag but gave up. He might even have confessed there were some papers in it that Song had asked for. Kang sighed and let Park go.

"You're the one who never forgets to eat. How could you forget something like that?"

Kang's angry muttering rang loud and clear in Park's ears. In his seat, Park tried hard to picture Song's face. The only thing he could remember—barely—was that Song had bad breath.

*

The next morning, Park still couldn't recall Song's face. He tried hard to convince himself that he wasn't naturally good at remembering people's faces.

"What happened to your wedding ring?" his wife asked as he was leaving for work. It must have been in the bag.

"The ring is a big deal now?" Park replied irritably.

The thought of having to talk about the documents gave him a headache and that made him frown even more than usual. His frowning had become chronic. His wife looked at him incredulously. He pretended not to notice her anger and shut the front door behind him.

All the way to the office, he kept calling the Lost and Found. His calls frequently dropped, and even when he did get through, he had a bad connection. The bag never turned up. If it had been reported to the Lost and Found, they would have contacted him.

He would have to tell Song the documents were missing before it was too late.

A man approached Park waving.

He squinted to recognize the person in front of him. It was a man with a dark face covered in moles. He drew closer to Park and asked if he was all right, his voice rising at the end. Only then did Park recognize him as Kim. He hadn't recognized Song or Kim because of his headache. Or it could have been because he wasn't wearing his glasses. Would he be okay if his myopia were corrected? Park felt apologetic for some reason, so he changed the topic to the earthquake. Kim replied that he hadn't even noticed the ground shaking. Park smiled at Kim-with-the-anonymous-face, relieved he wasn't the only one who hadn't noticed the tremors.

That morning, they were to meet with a client. Two people escorted Park from the office entrance to the conference room. Park was confused because he couldn't distinguish their faces. Yesterday it was Song's face he couldn't recall, and today it had been Kim's. He wondered if his own face would be next.

Park tried desperately to distinguish between them. He'd been dealing with them for the past eight years, attending their weddings and their kids' first birthdays. He couldn't bring himself to ask their names. Park smiled, trying to hide his embarrassment as he apologized for missing yesterday's appointment. Then he explained the circumstances under which the unit price would have to be adjusted. Luckily, as he spoke, he was able to tell the two men apart. One had a habit of sniffling constantly. This was Kwon, who suffered headaches because of his rhinitis. The other was Jeong. He was taller than Kwon.

Park explained at length to Kwon and Jeong—whose faces he still couldn't distinguish—that it would be difficult to continue trading without an upward adjustment in price. They replied that the price they had was reasonable for the current market. Park nodded automatically, often not getting what they were saying because he was thinking about the missing documents. Unlike at the start of the meeting, now not recognizing their faces didn't seem so much of a problem. They spoke in a businesslike manner, occasionally changing the subject to break up the formal atmosphere. Over the course of their conversation, as they discussed many things, Park brought up the earthquake six times. The fourth time, Kwon and Jeong just looked at him and shook their heads, smiling. Not realizing he was repeating himself, Park brought it up yet again. The two replied that they hadn't noticed the earthquake either.

They didn't reach an agreement on the deal price. Neither Kwon nor Jeong had the power to make a decision, and it went without saying that neither did Park. As usual, Park ended the meeting by saying he would consult with his boss. Just as they were about to leave, he brought up the earthquake again.

"About that earthquake . . ."

Kwon and Jeong shook their heads from side to side as if they'd agreed about that earlier.

"It was a pretty strong quake, but I didn't realize it until I saw it on the news."

All three of them sighed deeply for some reason before they left the meeting room.

Back in the office, Park wrote a report for the marketing department.

When he raised his head, he could see into Song's office, and then he remembered the missing papers. Song was usually with a guest. When he was alone, he would be talking on the phone or looking at his computer monitor. Sometimes he would just sit in his chair and drowse. When he came back from a meeting, he would crumple up the newspaper or kick the door, and if that happened, Park would be too afraid to go in and tell him he'd lost the documents. Even if Song seemed to be in a good mood, it would be the same. He didn't want to ruin Song's mood with a lost document.

Park continued to call the Lost and Found. The clerk at the center told him that the more time passed, the harder it would be to find the bag.

"If someone had thought to return it, it would be here already."

It sounded to Park like the clerk wanted him to give up.

His coworkers kept coming over to Park to ask him what the heck he had lost. Park would say whatever came into mind. He told Choi he had lost the deed to his apartment. Surprised, Choi asked him why he was carrying a thing like that around, and he replied that he was thinking of selling his apartment. Choi told him not to worry, that losing the documents didn't mean he had lost the apartment. He told Shim he'd lost a laptop he'd bought only ten days ago. When Park claimed he'd lost one of these things, it felt like he really had lost it.

"You should have been more careful."

They would add this little remark at the end of whatever they said, as if they'd conspired ahead of time.

"Yes, I should have been more careful," Park muttered after them.

The wife will continue to insist on taking care of the baby. The dampness in the apartment won't go away. He would have to listen to the baby's squalling get worse and worse. When he saw his wife soothing the crying child, he was terrified she might not be the grown-up one. Most of all, Park was tormented by the thought he was useless because he had lost the documents. He enjoyed his life as an office worker. The days were routine, monotonous, repetitive. So was a week, a month, a year. The routine left him with no questions about what he was working for, what he wanted ultimately, whether he had any ambitions once, or what would come next. He simply got to work punctually, ate his meals according to schedule regardless of his appetite, and squeezed in time to take care of the many miscellaneous tasks that piled up. Over time, Park had also come to believe that compliant and conscientious workers like him would sustain and eventually develop the company.

After he stopped remembering people's faces, he stayed cooped up in his office even longer. He didn't have to struggle to recognize people there. No problems arose because he had forgotten faces. Everything had its place. If he couldn't remember a face or was confused, he could just quietly sneak over to that person's station. Whenever he had to sit in a meeting with no assigned seating or had coffee in the break room or bumped into someone in the hallway, he was careful not to cause himself embarrassment.

The male employees wore crisp, white shirts and blue or brown ties, making them all look alike from a distance. Uniformed employees were even harder to tell apart. They had nearly identical haircuts and wore similarly nondescript accessories.

Gradually, Park was able to recognize people by the way they spoke, the shape of their glasses, their hair, and their smell. Kim was the one whose face looked dark because he had so many moles. In the office, Kim wore acupressure slippers densely studded with little plastic spikes. The slippers made a sort of slapping sound every time they touched the floor. Choi was the one with the long torso and the small, weak voice. He had a thick head of curly hair with a bald spot. Shim, who wore black-rimmed glasses, always smelled of tobacco, and his cigarettes were more mentholated than the ones Kang smoked. Kang always wore a rumpled white shirt because his wife and son were out of the country. He smelled like old laundry. Park would sit with his coworkers, whom he could only distinguish by their smells or voices, sharing their little jokes and sometimes getting swept up in the group making faces and criticizing Kang or Song. There were times when he'd call someone by the wrong name because he didn't recognize their face, but misspeaking someone's name was a common mistake, so Park's faux pas didn't stand out.

On the way back from lunch, Park asked Han and Choi if it wasn't strange no one seemed to know about the big earthquake. Han replied that it was because no one thought about the possibility of an earthquake. Choi, on the other hand, asked whether it wasn't more surprising people *had* thought it was an earthquake. Park felt obliged to reply that that seemed to be the case. Just then, his cell phone rang as if in response to his reply.

"Are you busy?"

It was Song.

"No."

Park's voice grew incredibly loud. At the sound of it, someone gave him a dark look, and for the first time, Park was fearful because he couldn't tell who it was. He felt as if aftershocks he couldn't perceive were still happening somewhere.

Someone looked at Park as he was going to Song's office and asked with concern, "Is something wrong?"

Park was in a rush—he didn't recognize the person. It could have been Kim, who'd patted him on the shoulder earlier, or it could have been Han.

There was only one person in Song's office. Park felt relieved.

"Been busy lately?" Song asked.

Park leaned closer to him. Song's breath smelled terrible.

"No." Park shook his head.

"All right. You can go now," Song said after a long while.

Park slowly stood up from his seat and sneaked a glance at Song. Wouldn't it be better even now to tell him the documents were lost? Song was reaching for his phone with a stony expression. Park closed the door carefully. It thudded quietly like Park's heart.

*

Behind the clerk who went to collect the bag, the shelves were stuffed full of lost and found items. All those things, once so precious to someone, looked dirty and shabby, like garbage. The clerk brought Park's bag from the lower shelf. The old strap barely supported it. The bag had been found the previous night in a station bathroom seven stops from where Park's office was located. The bag smelled of disinfectant. The clerk said it had been dumped in the bathroom trash can.

"Why the hell did it take so long to clean the bathroom?" Park wailed.

The clerk had an incredulous look on his face. Park took the empty bag in a huff and went back to his office. If he went home, the baby would probably be there.

Everyone had already left, and the office was quiet. Park's footsteps echoed through the empty space. There was an announcement posted from the end of the work day. Han was being promoted. Kang was being promoted and transferred to another department. Song had also posted an announcement for a party in recognition of all these exciting achievements.

*

Han and Kang would be embarrassed and try to lighten the mood by offering to buy a round. By now, they should all be drunk, clapping and singing happily. The thought that they might be actually enjoying themselves made Park a bit uncomfortable.

He slumped in his chair. He tried picking up his black bag by the frayed strap. The handle was worn, but its fit felt good in his hand. It would have been better if the bag hadn't been found. Now that it had, he was afraid the documents might turn up any time.

Park stuffed the empty bag into the office trash can. The papers were somewhere. They weren't needed by anyone but Song and Park. There was no point in telling Song the truth. Song had plenty of underlings, and they would always follow his orders. On the verge of tears, Park suddenly remembered Song's face. It was unmistakably Song, with his mouth firmly shut and his eyes in a squint. Park took out a notepad so as not to forget the face that had surfaced in his memory. But he wasn't good at drawing. He wouldn't be able to recognize the person from the drawing alone.

So he jotted down the face's distinctive features. In his memory, the face began to grow darker and darker. Eyes small and slightly upturned, forehead somewhat narrow, the bridge of the nose high but nostrils large, nose crooked, lips drooping and appearing angry. He stared at his notes for a long time. From them alone, he couldn't be sure it was Song.

On impulse, Park dialed Song's number. After a long signal, Song answered. Park heard loud singing in the background.

"I lost my bag!" he exclaimed.

"What?" Song shouted.

Park continued in a slightly louder voice. Song didn't respond. It was only then that Park regretted he'd made a mistake.

"What bag?" Song asked again after a long pause.

Park said it was a black bag with a worn-out strap.

"There are scratches here and there. The lock is broken, so it doesn't lock very well. Someone took it while I was asleep," he rambled on.

"Who stole it?" Song asked.

Someone started singing a new song. Several people were laughing in the background.

"It wasn't stolen. I forgot my bag when I got off."

Song didn't say anything. Park said all the documents were in the bag.

"What documents are you talking about?" Song asked after another long pause.

Park explained what the documents were, but he was incoherent. He was worried Song would hang up on him.

The sound of Song's sighs mixed with the melody coming out of the phone.

"I see." Song seemed about to hang up.

"But did you know there was a major earthquake the other night?" Park shouted, afraid the line would go dead.

Song hung up without a response. Park quietly set down his phone.

The office went silent. Park remained motionless sitting in his chair. He found it hard to read the notes he had scribbled on the paper. He closed his eyes and calmly studied the image of the face that rose up in his mind. He couldn't tell if it was the same face he had described in the notes. It could be Song or it could be Kim. It could have been someone he'd passed on the street once, or it could have been the face of an actor he'd seen on television. It could have been Park's own face. Darkness slowly spread over the faint image of the face. Park frowned. His head was aching.

—Translated by Heinz Insu Fenkl

COMMEMORATION

He lifted the large box and, hugging it to his chest, walked slowly into the apartment building. All the lights were turned off as if for the monthly blackout drill. The only light was the flashing red floor number above the elevator reflecting off the mailboxes. The building was just being vacated, but the scattered assortment of flyers, unclaimed mail, and empty cans stuffed into mailboxes made it seem as if demolition were already underway.

He turned toward the stairs. It was best not to take the elevator. There were frequent outages because the electricity was unreliable. He had once been stuck in the elevator with his deliveries, and no matter how many times he'd pressed the emergency call button, no custodian had shown up—just waiting for the demolition crew might have been faster. Exhausted, he'd fallen asleep hoping the elevator wouldn't crash, and it wasn't until the next morning that power had been restored.

Whenever he climbed the dark stairs, it felt like he was performing a magic trick that separated the upper and lower halves of his body. Even when he had to open his eyes wide to make out the steps, his legs would maintain the appropriate stride. He knew

155

how many sets of stairs connected one floor to the next in this building, the width of each stair, and which floor had the emergency exit where a bicycle had been dumped. Even so, he sometimes stumbled on the piles of trash. Every day there was more trash by the emergency exits.

He sat down on the stairs leading to the fifth floor. With all the lights out, the stairwell was pitch black. He tried shaking his last delivery, which was in a tall box, but there was no sound nor any smell or trace of leakage. One time he'd left a trail of red droplets wherever he went. The liquid had stained his khaki pants and even left an odor. He'd kept climbing the dark stairs as the wet spots on the floor slowly faded.

He delivered something to apartment 607 at least once a week. Some days it was kimchi, soybean paste, or hot red pepper paste. There were even times he'd delivered the kind of instant noodles you could buy at any supermarket. He'd also delivered sandals, Western-style leather boots, a steam cleaner with a long hose, and high-top sneakers. Items ordered by the woman in apartment 607 from home shopping or online sites passed through several staging points before being handed off to his delivery service.

The air was laden with concrete dust. It had been like that in the city ever since they'd started construction on the amusement park. The amusement park was being built on the other side of the river that cut through the city, facing the apartments on this side. Construction had been going on for the past four years, though from a distance it was hard to tell whether it was new construction or demolition that was actually taking place on the site. Tower cranes loomed like signs announcing the amusement park, and cargo containers used as temporary offices were placed at various corners like trash bins. Workers wearing yellow safety helmets swarmed the site constantly while trucks sped along the roads that bordered it, slowly sloughing off construction debris.

Noise and dust from new construction were constant, but it wasn't just the amusement park. The entire city was under construction; buildings would go up in just a month and apartment complexes would be demolished in a matter of days. Neighborhoods were slowly being replaced by apartment blocks. The noisy construction, with barrier walls, traffic cones, and workers in hard hats, had become a familiar sight in the alleyways he passed every day. The completion of the apartments and the opening of the amusement park wouldn't change that. Somewhere, a building would become dilapidated, and then the owner would take it down and rebuild it for the market value.

He accidentally kicked something, and there was the sharp sound of glass shattering. A cat startled by the noise darted out of an apartment and ran to the end of the hallway. He set down the package to catch his breath. The number plate had fallen off, and he couldn't tell whether it was 4 or 5. He peered into the apartment through the open door. The belongings and trash left behind looked like darker stains in the darkness.

The building was slated for a complete renovation. Not just a change to the exterior walls and a fresh coat of paint, as he would have thought. According to the notice, everything but the structural framework and the number of units was going to be changed. They would be replacing all the old utilities and wiring as well. When it had first gone up, this building and the telephone poles were the tallest things in the area. But it was twenty-nine years since it had been built. By the time construction was finished on the neighboring apartment buildings and people started moving in, this building would look even older. As he came to make his deliveries, he had witnessed the residents leaving one by one because of the renovation. For three years, they would be living in basic accommodations and then would move back into totally transformed apartments.

The doorbell to 607 didn't ring. Down in the lobby, the elevator lights had been flashing, but it appeared the electricity had cut out while he'd groped his way up six flights of stairs. He knocked on the metal door, relieved now that he hadn't taken the elevator. There was no response from inside.

"Anybody home?" he shouted, pressing his ear against the door.

He had been making deliveries to 607 for more than a year, and there was hardly a time when the woman who lived there hadn't been in. He took out his cell phone and called the number on the invoice. He couldn't hear any sound from the other side of the metal door. Using his phone for light, he read the description of the item on the invoice: a potted rubber plant. He worried if it might have gotten ruined because he'd been lifting it and putting it down carelessly. Once, he'd had to refund the woman for delivering cosmetics that were damaged. The bottles had broken in transit due to poor packaging, but he'd given her a refund anyway, though technically it was the seller's responsibility.

He decided to leave the box in the hallway. After all, 607 was the only occupied apartment left on the sixth floor. There were other residents on the other floors still, but no one would come and take a box left out in the hall. There was trash everywhere, and a box with a plant in it would look like trash too, he thought. He tightened his grip on the box in his arms. If there were other deliveries for 607 later, though, he could bring both. If the plant died in the meantime, there was nothing he could do about it. He headed back toward the stairs, where he was met with an acrid, damp smell as if from an incinerator.

*

He had to work later than usual because he had to make a stop at the warehouse. He'd wanted to come back to the neighborhood that afternoon, but it wasn't possible. There weren't many packages to deliver there since most of the residents had left, and the apartment complex was at some distance from the other area he was responsible for.

To pick up packages from the warehouse, he had to go all the way back, and it was physically exhausting. He'd tried to adjust his route many times, but it was no use. Because he had to go back and forth between the warehouse, the shipping center, and his extensive delivery area, he didn't finish work until 10:00 p.m.

The photo studio was still lit up even at this late hour. The photographer came out from the back room when he heard the tinkle of the bell that hung from the door. He greeted the man with a glance and went straight to the camera.

They were classmates from elementary school, and they'd lived all their lives in the city, though most of their schoolmates had moved away as adults. Those who couldn't leave had set up households and found jobs or started their own businesses. They'd all had high hopes for the new construction in the city, the photographer among them, and he was just like the rest.

There would be even more deliveries when apartment construction was finished and people began moving in. He knew that would be a good thing, but it depressed him to think he'd have to keep making deliveries all day long. His van was always crammed full of boxes as burdensome as his future. It felt like the packages and their assorted contents were pressing down on him. If he could have gotten back the insurance deposit he paid the shipping company, he would have quit right away, but that was impossible as long as they held on to it. Maybe after the new city was established—but then, who would want to move to the outer fringes of the city and put down an insurance deposit just to take on delivery work?

"You're still here? I was wondering what I'd do if you'd already left."

He dragged a chair from the corner and sat down. He knew the photographer went home only around midnight.

"It's always like this. It's all right."

While the photographer looked through the lens, he straightened his clothes, then lowered his glasses to the tip of his nose and stretched his shoulders wide to level them. Last time, he'd been told his right shoulder was too high.

"Relax your shoulders a bit."

He'd spread his shoulders, but now he let them sag again.

"You want me to take it like this today?"

Afraid his glasses might slide off his nose, he replied with a short affirmative grunt instead of nodding his head. The photographer started counting out loud. At "three" the flash went off.

While he waited for the photos to develop, he sat back in the chair and flipped through magazines.

"How are things at work?" the photographer asked.

Although they were classmates, they were actually only

acquaintances and had never had a real conversation before. Usually, as he waited for his pictures, he would read one of the vapid weekly magazines while the photographer was in the dark-room in the back.

"There's no place I haven't been to in this neighborhood," he said, smiling a little to hide his disappointment at his answer, which was uninteresting even to him.

"I was thinking of maybe looking for another job," the photog-rapher said. "I'd let my wife run the shop. Business has slowed down a lot, so she could handle it by herself."

"What were you thinking of doing?"

"I'll have to figure that out, I guess."

He was quiet for a moment, then asked, "What about delivery work?"

"Is it something I can start right away? That would be great."

"Not right away . . . But if you want, I can find out for you," he answered after deliberately dragging out the pause.

"Then I'd owe you one," the photographer said.

He took more interest than usual in the magazine. He'd real-ized he might be able to get his deposit back by transferring it to the photographer, and he didn't want to show any sign of excite-ment. He couldn't appear too eager to get the photographer the job right away or go on too long about the working conditions. If he seemed too eager, he could screw it up, and if he exaggerated, he'd raise suspicions.

"What are you going to use these photos for?" the photogra-pher asked.

He came just about every week to get a headshot in some odd pose.

"They're mementos."

"Mementos?"

He nodded emphatically. The photographer chuckled as he took the money. "How many occasions can you commemorate, anyway?"

Writing the date on the back of the photo, the man answered as if he'd been thinking about it for a long time, "Isn't every day worth commemorating?"

But even as he said it, he realized he actually had no memorable days to speak of. The only one he remembered was the anniversary of the day his parents had both died in an accident. They had been at the side of the road examining the bumper of their car after it had broken down when they'd been struck by another car. He had been just out of his teens then. It wasn't the sort of day to commemorate. He didn't have any family to celebrate his birthday in his parents' place. He didn't have a girlfriend to count the days with until they reached the hundredth-day anniversary of when they first met. He didn't want to celebrate the day he'd started his job or holidays like Christmas and New Year's. Days like that just doubled his workload.

He would attach the ID photos to his resume. On his days off, he always composed at least ten resumes. He would list his education, which had ended with high school, and the short-term work experience he'd had at several companies. Then, with a glue stick, he'd attach a headshot on the back of the page. He tried to make his photo appear as silly as possible. It was better to look ridiculous than pitiful. He sent all the completed resumes to companies in big cities.

Most of the time, he never heard back. He already knew that sending a handwritten resume in this day and age was a bad idea, but he still wrote them out by hand as if he were keeping a diary. Some days, he'd list the items he'd delivered that week, even including the name of the city he was delivering in. He even wrote down the names of the apartment buildings that would be built in the new city and listed the various brands of cup noodles he'd bought at the local supermarket.

There were times when he'd list credentials that were useless or irrelevant. He liked the sound the typewriter made, pattering like raindrops. When he was taking an exam once, he had been so nervous his fingers kept slipping between the keys. For his math certification, he'd struggled with problems involving combinations of two- and three-digit numbers. He would sometimes copy the figures off the test paper and calculate the solution on an abacus before writing down the answer.

But that was a long time ago. He didn't need those credentials anymore. He knew he couldn't get a job in the city with his resume. He could send out even more resumes, and the results would be the same.

He would always be an outsider. Sometimes it was comforting to think that when the new city was finished, the place where he lived might look like it belonged. On the other hand, he was ashamed to think that his living conditions, a room in a half-basement, were unlikely to improve. It didn't change anything. Neither shame nor security would change his life.

*

He set a small box containing a bottle of grapeseed oil on top of the one that held the potted rubber plant. He couldn't see very well, but it was dark so it didn't make any difference. At night, there was a faint dust haze on the stairs, like sighs exhaled by the old walls.

"Anyone there?!" he shouted, banging on the closed door.

His voice echoed in the empty hallway. He called the number on the invoice, but there was no answer. Maybe the woman had already left. The sign at the building entrance had announced the start date for interior demolition. Everyone had abandoned their old apartments, only at different times.

He looked down at the two boxes, puzzled. He knocked on the door again, wondering how long the woman planned to hold out in an apartment that was due for demolition if she was still ordering potted plants. Apart from the sound of plastic bags flapping in the draft at the end of the hallway, the apartment was eerily silent.

As he was turning to leave, he absentmindedly twisted the knob and the door swung open.

"Anyone there?"

He hid his surprise and stood just inside the door, raising his voice cautiously. There was no response from within. He picked up the boxes and looked around the apartment. Everything was still in place, suggesting the woman had just gone out for a while.

As he was turning to leave, suddenly light came flooding in, illuminating the room in an instant. The light was from the balcony off the living room and lit up every corner of the apartment like a searchlight. A greasy frying pan sat on the gas range in the kitchen. By the door was a pair of sandals—ones he might have delivered.

Mesmerized, he followed the brilliant light to the window. It emanated from a gigantic moving circle that slowly rotated, glowing with color after color as it shone into the woman's apartment from the amusement park across the river. The surface of the water sparkled and shimmered with light as the giant circle seemed to turn beneath it.

He had to stare for a long while before he realized the lights were from a Ferris wheel. The amusement park hadn't held its grand opening yet—maybe they were operating the rides to test them. He had never been on a Ferris wheel before. When his parents were alive, they had always been exhausted just trying to make ends meet. Even when they did have the money and time, there would have been no Ferris wheel on the outskirts where they lived. And their family was never the type to go on holiday outing to some distant amusement park. When he was older, an amusement park was no longer something rare or hard to get to, and he had gone occasionally with friends. He'd been on roller coasters that went more than sixty miles an hour and rides where he was dangling upside down and spun around on rails. A Ferris wheel was boring by comparison, not the kind of ride that crowds of people would line up for. No sense of speed, no thrill of heaven and earth turning upside down. It was a slow, boring ride, like his life, rising just high enough to offer a bird's-eye view of the city's gridlocked apartment complexes.

*

When he got home, he opened the boxes addressed to apartment 607. He'd brought them home even though he was required to return unclaimed items after a certain period of time.

The woman still wasn't answering his calls. A few days ago, he'd gone back to the apartment to deliver a package, just in case.

He hadn't been able to enter the building because workers had started demolishing the interior. So he imagined the woman in apartment 607 must have disappeared, leaving him all at once the gifts he'd never received in his life. It was only by imagining it that way that he could go ahead and open the boxes. He even felt the excited anticipation people had when they opened presents. On his wall calendar, he itemized the boxes' contents: a potted rubber plant, a bottle of grapeseed oil, a set of pots won in a sweepstakes, a set of seven kitchen knives including a knife rack, a bamboo floor mat, and a pillow stuffed with chrysanthemum petals.

It was fun to think of uses for things—he preferred surprise gifts to ones that had been thought out for their usefulness or in anticipation of his tastes. He put the rubber plant outside to block the window and hide the feet of passersby.

He used the grapeseed oil to fry eggs and sauté potatoes. The choice of grapeseed oil suggested that the woman was either health-conscious or susceptible to fads. Although he didn't cook, even he knew there were fads when it came to food. In the set of pots from the sweepstakes, the wide-bottomed one was big enough to use as a wash basin. His plastic basin had cracked, and he was going to buy a new one anyway. He put the bamboo mat on his floor. It was getting cold, so he put a quilt on top of it. He didn't know why anyone would buy a bamboo floor mat when summer had already ended. Maybe the woman in 607 was unusually hot-blooded. At school, there had been a kid in his class nicknamed "Summer Shorts" because he was always the first to wear them and the last to stop wearing them in the fall. He tried the same nickname for the woman in 607: Summer Shorts.

Once, he had two deliveries of the same item, a wide-brimmed hat. The first one was pink, but a few days later an identical one came in blue. The woman must have liked the hat so much she'd bought the same item in a different color. He gave the second one to his landlady, who asked where she could possibly wear a hat like that. But she ended up liking it so much she wore it whenever she was supervising the contractors.

The multifamily house where he lived was being renovated, too. It was originally two stories, but it was being increased to four and the exterior walls were being repaired. When he opened the window, a cloud of cement dust and sand blew in on the breeze. Even with all the doors and windows shut, he could see the dust that settled on his black TV set. Loud drilling shook the house. When he was lying in bed, the sound would make him queasy. Sometimes he couldn't stand it and threw his pillow at the ceiling. The fluorescent lights would sway wildly and the nausea-inducing noise wouldn't stop until night.

Now he was thinking he would give the set of seven knives to the photographer's wife. The photographer had come to the shipping center and shadowed him for a few days of training. When they were together, he would finish his rounds by 7:00 p.m., and the photographer was pleased to see work ended earlier than expected.

He avoided lying to the photographer by saying it wasn't always like that. He didn't tell him he'd delivered the remaining items after the photographer had gone home. The photographer would realize he'd been lied to only after he quit, but by then he would also understand there'd been no other option.

He took all the headshots he kept for his resume out of the drawer and spread them on the floor. The length of his hair and the clothes he wore were different in each, but it was always the same ridiculous face. He tried arranging them in chronological order without looking at the dates written on the back. It was easy to tell which photo was the oldest and which was the most recent. The rest were hard to put in order without consulting the dates. It was difficult to guess, from the slightly different expressions, what he must have been thinking or how he was feeling on the day a particular photo was taken. He looked at his old faces for a long time, unable to determine anything.

From among the photos he picked one that had been taken the previous winter in which he was wearing a black turtleneck and looked haggard. He had probably just been tired. His days then were exhausting, and he'd suffered from migraines while driving. In the photo, his hair was longer than it was now. He cut his hair out of the photo. He snipped out the eyes from a photo taken last summer. Those bloodshot eyes—he remembered having that picture taken. He'd gotten conjunctivitis from someone at the shipping center. Tears kept dripping from his inflamed eyes, and the rims had been thick with puslike mucus. The photographer had laughed, asking if he really wanted a photo with his eyes in that condition.

He snipped the ears off a photo taken two years ago. Because his hair was short in it, his ears angled downward with the lobes hardly showing. He glued the cutout hair, eyes, and ears onto the photo he'd had taken with his glasses pushed down to the tip of his nose. The resulting picture looked too small, and he was too clumsy with the scissors to fix the design. When he glued on the cutout hair, his hair looked bushy instantly. His red eyes were huge, and the sharp ears poked like goblins' horns through the top of his bushy hair. That was the photo he glued onto his resume.

*

The woman from apartment 607 asked to meet at the amusement park, which was still being readied for opening. It wasn't until he heard the address that he realized it was the same woman. When she told him she'd had a hard time finding him, he looked around at all her things in his room.

The rubber tree, covered in construction dust, was dying. It looked like no amount of watering could revive its parched roots. Dried and yellow leaves had fallen to the floor like dust. Because the season had changed, his landlady no longer wore her hat though the construction work still wasn't finished. The pot he used as a wash basin was scratched and scuffed from the bathroom tiles. The grapeseed oil was already more than half used up. The bamboo mat, packed with dust in every crevice, lay like sheetrock under the thick quilt. He would eat ramen and clip his finger- and toenails on the uncovered mat. At night, he would fall asleep on the pillow stuffed with chrysanthemum petals. The pillow was indented in the middle with a depression made by the back of his head. He finally stopped imagining all these things had been gifts. He would have to go to the woman from 607, apologize to her, and reimburse her for all the merchandise.

Though the park wasn't open yet, the rides were already running. The red rollercoaster sped endlessly along the rails at more than sixty miles per hour. It was dizzying to watch, and even though he knew he would never fall off, he held his breath until it returned to its destination.

The Ferris wheel was at the very back of the amusement park. The woman standing at the entrance recognized him from his uniform. She said they should go inside a gondola since there was nowhere else to sit. He stepped in time with the slowly moving Ferris wheel and followed her into the gondola that arrived in front of them. The woman clicked a stopwatch the moment they got in.

"I need to check the running time," she said.

He turned and looked out the window. The Ferris wheel was set to turn at a constant speed, but each revolution was slightly different. One after the other, the gondolas dangled from the ends of what looked like the spokes on a bicycle wheel. The gondolas swayed gently in the wind. It was slow, but it was definitely moving away from the ground.

"I'm sorry," he said, bowing his head as he sat there.

"There's nothing you could have done about it anyway," the woman said.

Her tone was more subdued than her initial outburst when she'd demanded that he bring the items back.

He told her he would total up the cost of the goods and pay her the full price.

The woman nodded wordlessly with a look of acknowledgment and continued watching the time.

He studied her furtively. He'd delivered packages to her practically every week. For a face he'd seen so often, it was as unfamiliar as if she were a total stranger.

He exhaled loudly and turned his gaze to the window. They

were slowly moving away from the construction site. He could see all the empty rides constantly spinning. Their massive bodies twisted and turned with loud mechanical cries. As the gondola rose higher, he could see the woman's apartment building across the river. It was brightly lit, as if construction would be continuing all night. From the twinkling lights, one couldn't tell that it had been gutted on the inside and reduced to a skeleton. The neighboring buildings, also under construction, were the gray color of cement—like dying trees driven into the ground. If they climbed higher, he might be able to spot the multifamily housing complex where he lived. He wanted to see even farther. Until he could look down on the messy tangle of roads that were like knife cuts leading to other cities. He stood up too quickly and hit his head on the ceiling. He had to stoop as they lurched to a stop somewhere in the middle.

He looked at the woman's expressionless face and suddenly wanted to ask her what she liked. Whether she liked the heat, whether she hated that she looked short enough to wear platform sneakers. He wanted to tell her she wasn't really that short. He wanted to ask if she'd noticed how beautifully the Ferris wheel lit up her apartment at night. But he kept his mouth shut, wondering at the restless questions that kept coming to mind. It was because he felt he might let everything spill out without realizing it.

The earth glowed magnificently as it coalesced into a great mass of light. There he was in his truck, endlessly hauling parcels to people he didn't know. Making deliveries all day long, his face as stiff as a cardboard box. There, too, was the photographer snapping photos of people, their faces expressionless or the corners of their lips slightly raised. The photographer would trim the stiff headshots as he pulled them out of the printer one after the other. An image of his landlady also appeared wearing her wide-brimmed hat, dozing off as she sat at a construction site. Then there was the woman, by the locked door of the Ferris wheel gondola, forever staring at her stopwatch to check the running time. He waved to them all.

As if in response to his gesture, fast-paced, upbeat music suddenly began to play. A cheerful recording announced that the Ferris wheel had reached the top. He was surprised when he heard it was 541 feet. He marveled at how the ground could look so beautiful when they were only that high up. Now the Ferris wheel slowly descended, still spinning as slowly as the earth.

"I gave the hat to my landlady," he said quickly, while she was looking out the window.

She responded with a short "Is that so?" After a moment, she became expressionless again and asked, "What kind of hat is it?"

"It has a wide brim. The front's a little curved, and there's a little ribbon tied in the back."

He traced the contours of the brim with his hand. She followed his fingertips as if she could see the hat floating in the air.

The date by which he was supposed to receive the money for the deposit had passed, but he hadn't heard from the photographer. He was getting anxious but hadn't called. Maybe he would end up getting hold of the photographer and begging him to give him the money right away. The longer he waited, the harder it would be to get his deposit back. He would end up not being able to leave the outer fringes, and every day he'd have to drive to every single corner of a city under perpetual construction. With that thought, he pulled his resume out of his pocket and, while the woman was looking away, slipped it into a narrow gap in the Ferris wheel seat. One corner of the resume stuck out like a white flag. It would go round and round forever on the Ferris wheel. On a clear day, he might even be able to see distant cities through those red eyes. But mostly, he'd get a bird's-eye view of the whole city under construction.

The Ferris wheel didn't come to a complete stop when it touched down but continued to inch forward. He felt slightly dizzy when his feet finally stood on the ground. He steadied himself and bowed politely to the woman. She thrust a piece of paper at him with a list of the items on it. She had listed the price of each item she hadn't received.

"How long did it take to go around?" he asked, accepting the list and putting it in his pocket.

The woman looked at the stopwatch and told him it was a bit faster than usual.

He left the woman and walked back to the entrance to the amusement park. There were packages for her in his van. He didn't know what the items were because he hadn't checked the invoice, so he hadn't told her they were there. Maybe she wasn't even the one who'd ordered them. He could deliver them once he'd reimbursed her. In the future, he would come to the Ferris wheel to deliver her things.

As he left the amusement park, he turned to look back at the Ferris wheel. It was carrying no one all lit up, and yet it still spun slowly, illuminating the dark city in the night as if the world would stop spinning if it did.

He tried to find the gondola he'd just gotten out of, but in the tangled mass of light it was hard to make out the one with his resume in it. The boxes in the luggage racks rattled a bit as he climbed into his van and drove off into the night with his packages.

—Translated by Heinz Insu Fenkl